Banished from the Hero's Party, I Decided to Live a Quiet Life in the Countryside

9

ZAPPON

Illustration by Yasumo

"I finally found you."

Van of Flamberge

A second Hero. Prince of a country destroyed by the demon lord's army. He's on a rampage and determined to defeat Ruti.

"…"

CONTENTS

Prologue **The Hero Never Wavers**
001

Chapter 1 **Hero Countermeasures**
003

Chapter 2 **Targeting the Fairy in Love and the Greedy Cardinal**
047

Chapter 3 **And Sometimes I'm Not Sure**
079

Chapter 4 **Confusion and Then Rampage**
091

Chapter 5 **The Hero's Challenge**
133

Epilogue **Conclusion, and the Next Journey**
153

Afterword
165

Illustration: Yasumo
Design Work: Shindousha

"Thanks for the purchase!"

"I don't think I'll be able to forget, either."

Escarlata Dias (Esta)

Theodora in disguise. Hired to support Van the Hero because of her strength and experience. A masked warrior stunned by her abrupt, late-blooming first love.

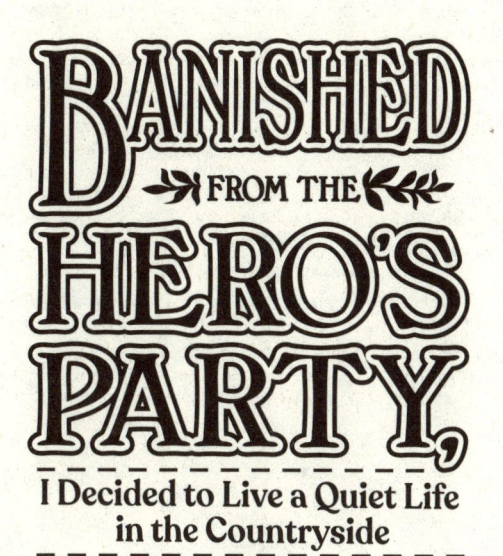

Banished from the Hero's Party,

I Decided to Live a Quiet Life in the Countryside

9

ZAPPON

Illustration by Yasumo

Yen On

New York

Banished from the Hero's Party, I Decided to Live a Quiet Life in the Countryside, Vol. 9
Zappon

Translation by Dale DeLucia
Cover art by Yasumo

▼▼▼▼▼▼▼▼▼▼▼▼▼▼▼

This book is a work of fiction. Names, characters, places, and incidents are the product of the author's imagination or are used fictitiously. Any resemblance to actual events, locales, or persons, living or dead, is coincidental.

SHIN NO NAKAMA JYANAI TO YUUSHA NO PARTY WO OIDASARETANODE, HENKYOU DE SLOW—LIFE SURUKOTO NI SHIMASHITA Vol. 9
©Zappon, Yasumo 2021
First published in Japan in 2021 by KADOKAWA CORPORATION, Tokyo.
English translation rights arranged with KADOKAWA CORPORATION, Tokyo through TUTTLE-MORI AGENCY, INC., Tokyo.

English translation © 2023 by Yen Press, LLC

Yen Press, LLC supports the right to free expression and the value of copyright. The purpose of copyright is to encourage writers and artists to produce the creative works that enrich our culture.

The scanning, uploading, and distribution of this book without permission is a theft of the author's intellectual property. If you would like permission to use material from the book (other than for review purposes), please contact the publisher. Thank you for your support of the author's rights.

Yen On
150 West 30th Street, 19th Floor
New York, NY 10001

Visit us at yenpress.com
facebook.com/yenpress
twitter.com/yenpress
yenpress.tumblr.com
instagram.com/yenpress

First Yen On Edition: July 2023
Edited by Yen On Editorial: Jordan Blanco
Designed by Yen Press Design: Andy Swist

Yen On is an imprint of Yen Press, LLC.
The Yen On name and logo are trademarks of Yen Press, LLC.

The publisher is not responsible for websites (or their content) that are not owned by the publisher.

▼▼▼▼▼▼▼▼▼▼▼▼▼▼▼

Library of Congress Cataloging-in-Publication Data
Names: Zappon, author. | Yasumo, illustrator. | DeLucia, Dale, translator.
Title: Banished from the hero's party, I decided to live a quiet life in the countryside / Zappon ; illustration by Yasumo ; translation by Dale DeLucia ; cover art by Yasumo.
Other titles: Shin no nakama ja nai to yuusha no party wo oidasareta node, henkyou de slow life suru koto ni shimashita. English
Description: First Yen On edition. | New York : Yen On, 2020.
Identifiers: LCCN 2020026847 | ISBN 9781975312459 (v. 1 ; trade paperback) | ISBN 9781975312473 (v. 2 ; trade paperback) | ISBN 9781975312497 (v. 3 ; trade paperback) | ISBN 9781975312510 (v. 4 ; trade paperback) | ISBN 9781975333423 (v. 5 ; trade paperback) | ISBN 9781975343248 (v. 6 ; trade paperback) | ISBN 9781975343262 (v. 7 ; trade paperback) | ISBN 9781975343286 (v. 8 ; trade paperback) | ISBN 9781975350536 (v. 9 ; trade paperback)
Subjects: CYAC: Ability—Fiction. | Fantasy.
Classification: LCC PZ7.1.Z37 Ban 2020 | DDC [Fic]—dc23
LC record available at https://lccn.loc.gov/2020026847

ISBNs: 978-1-9753-5053-6 (paperback)
978-1-9753-5054-3 (ebook)

10 9 8 7 6 5 4 3 2 1

LSC-C

Printed in the United States of America

CHARACTERS

Red (Gideon Ragnason)
Kicked out of the Hero's party, he headed to the frontier to live a slow life. Although not as powerful as Ruti, he's one of humanity's greatest swordsmen, with many feats to his name.

Rit (Rizlet of Loggervia)
The princess of the Duchy of Loggervia and a former adventurer hailed as a hero. Now she is a truly happy young woman who has grown out of her combative phase.

Ruti Ragnason
Red's younger sister and possessor of the Divine Blessing of the Hero, humanity's strongest blessing. Free at last from her blessing's impulses, she now enjoys life in Zoltan as a medicinal herb farmer while adventuring on the side.

Tisse Garland
A young girl with the Divine Blessing of the Assassin. An elite from the Assassins Guild, she is taking a break from her usual job and working with Ruti to get their medicinal herb farm running.

Yarandrala
A high elf Singer of the Trees capable of controlling plants. Brimming with endless curiosity, she has been through countless adventures during her long life.

Danan LeBeau
Humanity's strongest Martial Artist. He's overjoyed that he's finally done recovering. A natural musclehead who doesn't understand the concept of a slow life.

Albert Leland
Bears the Divine Blessing of the Champion and was once a hero in Zoltan. He now acts as Escarlata's squire. A reliable comrade to Red and his friends.

Cardinal Ljubo
One of the key figures of leadership in the holy church. A big man, well over two meters tall. Van the Hero's ambitious guardian.

Lavender
A small fairy. She met Van in a secret grove, fell in love with him, and pushed her way into the party. She is free-spirited and does not care about people. Van alone is special to her.

Prologue

The Hero Never Wavers

After a bloody, difficult struggle, pushing through countless soldiers' corpses, they finally reclaimed a country from the demon lord's army. Only to have it all stolen back in a single night by Desmond of the Earth.

While others fell into despair, Ruti the Hero continued walking forward without delay.

"Brother, how do we take it back again?" the Hero said to the knight beside her. She neither commiserated with the soldiers who hung their heads nor attempted to encourage them.

The Hero simply acted to save.

She was indomitable. Dauntless. The Hero always pushed ahead.

That was why people sought the Hero.

Even in the grip of pain and suffering, when their minds were fractured and their hearts broken, they believed that so long as they marched behind that girl, she would lead them to salvation.

The Hero never feels doubt.

The Hero must never waver.

All living creatures received Divine Blessings. Thus, no matter how terrible the betrayal, how terrible the beating, or how many lives lost, the Hero was never permitted to waver. Not to their final breath.

"Yes, that is the role expected of me."

When the new Hero, Van, heard the story of Ruti, his heart danced.

"Lord Demis, I am grateful for the trial you have set before me. May you continue to grant me greater challenges until my body, my essence, the comrades who walk alongside me, until all of it crumbles away."

He prayed from the depths of his heart, kneeling in the captain's room of the *Vendidad*, the demon lord's ship.

This chamber had once been the private quarters of a previous demon lord. Now it housed an altar Van the Hero had brought so he could offer his pious words to Demis.

Crew members outside the room sang a requiem for their comrade who'd perished to a monster.

Their voices were hoarse and tearful. Had Ruti been there, she would have been sad, but Van felt nothing. He didn't even remember the dead person's name.

Because the Hero never faltered.

Chapter 1

Hero Countermeasures

Three days had passed since Van the Hero and his comrades left for the south seas to increase their levels.

There was a chime as the shop door opened.

""Welcome!""

Rit and I called out in unison.

"Hey, Red!"

"Huh? What happened to the high elf lady?"

The half-elf carpenter Gonz and the half-orc furniture craftsman Stormthunder walked in.

"Your selection dropped while you were out, but looks like you've restocked pretty well," Gonz remarked as he eyed the shelves.

"I went to the mountains yesterday to gather some ingredients. A few herbs need to be dried first, so it will take a couple of days before we have everything we typically do."

"Oh? Look at this go-getter, workin' hard right after a vacation. I would've taken it easy for a few days at least."

Gonz guffawed as he grabbed some hangover medicine. Meanwhile, Storm gave Gonz a cold stare, but he also took some hangover medicine.

"Your stuff really is the best, you know. With this, I don't have to worry about drinking straight through the night."

Despite giving Gonz the stink eye, Storm hardly had any room to talk.

I smiled and then looked away.

"Still, what a shock for the Hero to come all the way out to Zoltan. Talk about a jerk, though."

Gonz picked up some cold medicine and a few disinfectants, too.

"Got that right." Storm nodded and grabbed three bags of medicinal cookies.

Yarandrala understood plenty about the effects of various medicinal herbs, but using a skill to turn them into medicine required a different sort of knowledge.

Thanks to all the work Rit and I put in, our apothecary was now a regular stop for lots of people.

Rit and I had returned from our vacation in Sant Durant to sold-out shelves and a drawer filled with order slips for medicines that had gone out of stock while we were gone.

The back-ordered items were all inexpensive commodities, but I was glad that goods made at our store were so important to people.

"Oh hey, why don't we go out drinking tomorrow?" Gonz put his chosen items on the counter. "A get-together to celebrate getting back from vacation."

"Oh, that'd be great. Let's hear some stories from your trip."

Storm leaned in with Gonz.

If it hadn't been for the current situation, I would've agreed in a heartbeat. However… "Sorry, I've gotta refuse. I'll be sure to let you guys know when I can make it."

"Really? All right. I'll be looking forward to it."

Gonz graciously accepted that answer.

It was the Zoltan way not to probe too deeply into personal matters. Storm looked like he wanted to say something more, but Gonz held out a hand to stop him and then smirked.

"So, how was your holiday with Rit?"

Zoltan folks didn't pry very much, but those in this part of town still loved their dirty stories.

Gonz had a lewd smirk on his handsome elven face, and behind him, Storm crossed his arms and flashed a grin.

Sheesh...

"That will have to wait, too," I said. "Once we're drinking, I'll talk until the grapes turn to wine."

"Hah-hah-hah, lookin' forward to it."

Another peaceful day in Zoltan.

✳   ✳   ✳

I headed over to Dr. Newman's clinic in Zoltan's working-class neighborhood.

"Red! It's been a while!"

Elenora the nurse sat at reception reading a book. She smiled upon seeing me.

"Good morning."

"Any souvenirs from your trip?"

"A few different types of dried river fish."

"Oh? I'm sure the doctor will enjoy them, but I'd prefer something sweet."

"I thought you might say that, so I also got a bottle of local apple juice."

"Yay!"

Elenora giggled.

"We sampled a bit during our stay, so I can vouch for the flavor."

"I can't wait. I'll try it with the doctor later."

Elenora stowed the package of dried fish and the bottle of apple juice in a basket typically kept beneath the counter.

This clinic accepted goods in addition to money. I saw some meat, some vegetables, a bundle of nails, and some metalwork in the basket.

Noticing my gaze, Elenora smiled and shrugged. "It'd be nice if he were a little more selective about what he took as payment. This wooden doll isn't nearly enough to cover the cost of treatment; he always insists things like this are enough."

"It's because everyone counts on Dr. Newman."

"Even so..."

"Hah-hah. It's fine." A warm voice cut Elenora off before she could complain more. "My clinic earns enough to live off of. And that metalwork will likely sell for more than the cost of a checkup, won't it?"

"Ugh! You're always like this!"

Dr. Newman, clad in his white coat, smiled at Elenora's reply.

"What? If we ever go hungry, I'm sure the kind people in the neighborhood will gladly treat us to some food. When people are in trouble, I help them; when I'm in trouble, they help me. This is a good town."

"Well, sure, but..."

"All right, enough of this. I have to take care of Red's medicine delivery."

Dr. Newman clapped his hands to end the conversation. Elenora let out a little sigh, acting exasperated, but grinned as she returned to her work.

She didn't usually act like she took her job very seriously, yet she undoubtedly respected Dr. Newman's approach to business.

"Now then, it's been a while, Red."

"Sorry for any trouble while I was away."

"It's no trouble at all. This is Zoltan. Even an apothecary and a doctor can take some time off when they need a break."

"You hardly ever take holidays, though."

"That's because I love my job."

Dr. Newman was one of the few exceptions to the general rule of Zoltan sloth. The man was no stick-in-the-mud, however. He'd spend evenings with Gonz and the others on occasion. He never indulged excessively, but he enjoyed his drinks all the same.

It was only natural that the people of the neighborhood loved him.

Depending on the timing of the seniority system, he might even wind up a part of the Zoltan council.

"...Mhm. It looks like all the medicine I ordered is here. And last year's blood needle deficit doesn't seem to be an issue anymore."

"The medicinal plants are all growing well this year. And we've got my sister's plantation, too. We'll have plenty of herbs to spare."

"That's great to hear."

After completing his review of the delivery, Dr. Newman offered me a cup of coffee.

That's rare.

"You can't really call Zoltan coffee luxurious, but I still like the flavor."

"Yeah, it's simple and has a nice feel to it."

We enjoyed the pleasant aroma that wafted with the white steam while sipping from our cups.

"Listen, about that Van boy..." Newman peered into the contents of his mug. "Do you think that he's really the Hero?"

"Cardinal Ljubo from the holy church is his guardian, and Father Clemens has acknowledged Van publicly, so I'm sure at least a handful of people have used Appraisal on him. Passing him off as the Hero after that would be difficult unless he was the genuine article."

"Hmmm..."

Van the Hero had humiliated Zoltan and endangered it by bringing salt dragons to wreak havoc. And when asked for an explanation, Van had made no attempt to disguise his motivation.

"If salt dragons destroy Zoltan, then its slothful people will be motivated to fight the demon lord's army."

Could he really not imagine how people would react when they heard that?

Van had a cardinal's backing, so no one would dare try to harm him. Still, the people of Zoltan had no interest in cooperating with him, either. The boy had brought the outrage on himself.

Van was fortunate that foreign crewmen who sailed the secondhand ships the Zoltan navy had bought to replace those lost fighting Veronia were still in town. The giant *Vendidad* operated on steam power, requiring fewer hands than a large galleon. I didn't know the exact number, but a ship that huge likely still needed dozens of people.

By gathering the foreign sailors drinking at the harbor while waiting for the next vessel out of Zoltan, Van managed to take the demon lord's ship to the south seas.

"Since he left, it's been dead quiet at every tavern in the harbor district," I said.

"According to one of my patients, no one's upset about that. Apparently, a lot of the guests were ill-mannered. Just between the two of us, I heard that straight from an inn owner." Newman shrugged. "Sure hope none of those sailors run afoul of Cardinal Ljubo on the voyage."

"...Have you met the cardinal before?" I asked.

Dr. Newman set his mug on the table and sighed.

"This was a long time ago, and from his perspective, I doubt I was anyone worth remembering...but yeah. We met when he was still a young inquisitor."

Ljubo had been an inquisitor before climbing the church ranks to become a cardinal. He'd served as an inquisitor at around the time I'd joined the Bahamut Knights, so I'd never interacted with him.

"To sum him up...well, I suppose he was a *reasonable* inquisitor."

"'A reasonable inquisitor'...?"

The look on Dr. Newman's face told me he didn't mean that in a positive way.

So that's it.

"I imagine he could live pretty comfortably like that."

"Hah-hah-hah..."

He was the sort of inquisitor who used his authority to take bribes.

Honestly, that sort was preferable to the self-righteous inquisitors who tortured people without any guild, but...

"The doctor who taught me the medical arts was quite poor. He was the sort who accepted a late payment once a patient recovered and had the money."

"And that's why you operate your clinic the way you do?" I asked.

"If anything, seeing how much he suffered left me careful to ensure I always get what I'm owed. He had bean soup for lunch every day. It wasn't even proper food if you ask me. I eat what I like, when I like."

Newman's face darkened. "Because he was poor, he had nothing to give Inquisitor Ljubo. And my teacher wasn't the type to keep quiet to get along with others. He believed anyone with the money for a bribe should use that wealth for treating the needy."

"I'm guessing that made him a target."

"That's right… Other doctors didn't appreciate that he treated patients for practically free. So a few of them paid Ljubo to get rid of him."

"How so?"

"Ljubo accused him of creating narcotics. Said that was how he kept his business running despite never getting paid. 'An action deviant from the Divine Blessing of the Doctor,' he called it. Ljubo took my teacher away, claiming he needed proper guidance. I can still see it all so clearly."

"What did they do to him?"

"His hands were cut off to keep him from making any more medicine."

"That's horrible…"

"'Now you can devote yourself to treating people, as one with the Doctor blessing ought to,' Ljubo said. It was awful…"

"What happened after?"

"By the time I arrived at the clinic the next day, my teacher had already left town. He left behind a medical document written in a barely legible scrawl. My guess is he wrote while holding the pen in his mouth. However, he remained true to his profession."

This was the first time Newman had spoken of his past with me.

I get why he wouldn't want to talk about it…

"I don't know what he's doing now. I hope he's alive somewhere… To be honest, part of the reason I came out to Zoltan was because I wondered if he might wander to a place like this, so removed from everything. Unfortunately, that hunch turned out to be wrong."

Newman took a sip of coffee, and his tense cheeks relaxed a bit.

"Sorry to talk your ear off. I suppose I can't help but worry a bit…"

"About Cardinal Ljubo and Van the Hero?"

"Ljubo punished an innocent man for money. I can't believe he'd devote himself for the sake of the Hero or the world."

So he's worried that the man who harmed his teacher might also threaten peace in Zoltan. I can't deny the possibility.

Ljubo surely didn't have any particular desire to destroy Zoltan, but judging by what Tisse said, he believed any mistakes Van made in Zoltan would serve as good learning experiences for the new Hero.

The fate of a tiny settlement in the middle of nowhere was a trivial thing to one of the church's highest-ranking members.

Can't say I like the idea of that.

"Red, you're different from me, right? You're not like the simple village doctor who couldn't do anything but run away from the inquisitor."

"I suppose so. I do at least have a little more experience fighting, and I've got some trustworthy comrades, too…and I don't have the power to save people who are sick, as you do. So yeah, I'd say we are a bit different."

"Then I suppose I'll do my best here as a doctor."

"Yeah, and I promise I'll do everything I can as well."

"Thank you, Red. It seems I've grown timid with age."

He smiled, as if a bit more hopeful, and I returned the expression.

"Another difference is I have a cute girlfriend while you're alone."

"Hah-hah-hah… You… Don't blame me if I hit you, okay?"

We laughed and enjoyed a pleasant conversation befitting a Zoltan afternoon.

I'd like to meet the doctor who taught him someday.

※　　　　　　※　　　　　　※

When a patient came in complaining of stomach pain, I took my leave.

The white petals of the blossoming sapphireberry trees lining the path were already starting to scatter. The foliage was shifting from spring to summer colors.

There was time yet until the hot months, but it looked like it'd be warmer than usual.

If so, everyone will just lie around.

"Four deliveries! Rush order!"

"Right away!"

A shopkeeper and his son who were peddling dyed goods called to each other. The boy, who was around fourteen, carried a big crate on his back, and his gait was unsteady as he rushed off. They'd lived in Zoltan longer than I had and appeared to know they wouldn't want to do any work this summer.

Everyone was working hard now so they could take it easy during the hot days.

"Let's get our blessing levels up to four this month!"

""Yeah!!!""

A group of three adventurers walked by, getting psyched up.

Hmm. A Warrior, a Cleric, and a Craftsman.

Most likely, they had other jobs and adventured on the side. They wore patched-up old armor as they headed out of town to hunt monsters. It had only been a few days since the dragon attack. Were they tough or just unconcerned?

"That's one of the good things about Zoltan," I muttered.

"Yes, I agree."

"Yarandrala!"

"Hi, Red! I hoped I'd bump into you!"

A smile bloomed on the high elf Yarandrala's face.

*   *   *

It was evening at Red & Rit's Apothecary.

"Thank you very much."

After seeing off the last customer, I closed up shop.

"Everything flew off the shelves today."

I'd restocked that morning, but the displays were looking barren already.

I'd need to pull an all-nighter to get our supplies ready.

I need to go to Ruti's plantation tomorrow.

"Mhm, come. My plantation is doing well. I'm sure we have what you need."

Ruti nodded beside me, copying how I crossed my arms on the counter.

"Sorry to interrupt while you're making plans for tomorrow..."

I turned around.

"Shall we go over what we've discovered so far and discuss our Hero countermeasures?"

Rit, Ruti, and I were assembled in the store, along with...

"All right, let's figure out how to kick that Hero jerk's ass!"

"You mean how we're going to run him out of Zoltan without fighting."

"Either way, he's a dangerous opponent."

...Danan, Yarandrala, and Tisse.

They were all comrades who'd fought alongside Ruti when she was still the Hero.

"Detect."

Yarandrala's spell enveloped us.

"There's no one spying on us or eavesdropping."

"And no one hiding the standard way, either," Tisse added.

Undoubtedly, no human could evade both Yarandrala and Tisse.

*   *   *

The living room.

Six world-class heroes sat around a table in the candlelit room.

"First of all, a final confirmation. Van's got no support nearby except his party members, right?" I said.

"No. Definitely not," Yarandrala answered.

Everyone else nodded.

"Cardinal Ljubo apparently expected to use church funds to purchase support from the Zoltan church and local adventurers," Tisse reported.

"We investigated all available lodgings and didn't find anyone in his pocket," Ruti explained.

"If there were anyone else, they would've shown up when Yarandrala and I were fighting him," Danan added.

Rit bobbed her head. "I asked around among the adventurers, and apparently, Van's party originally limited the request for crew on the *Vendidad* to C rank and above, but lowered it to D rank when they didn't get enough volunteers."

"If there were anyone else they could use, they wouldn't have made such a desperate move to recruit help," I said. That much was sure.

"At the very least, it's nice to know we only have to worry about the Hero's party."

"Yeah, the church's finest aren't to be trifled with."

The church was the largest organization on the continent. It recruited and trained some of the best around.

Before joining up with Ruti, Theodora had been a spear-fighting instructor for the church, and she hadn't even been the greatest warrior at the clergy's disposal at the time.

Considering how much she'd grown from fighting the demon lord's forces, I doubted anyone at the church could match her anymore, but that didn't make them any less formidable.

"Cardinal Ljubo probably intends to monopolize the glory from the Hero's achievements," I said.

"Either way, it makes our job easier."

I nodded at Rit's comment.

"So then, what about Van's comrades?" I asked.

"We know a bit thanks to Theo—Esta." Rit set three pieces of paper on the table. Each had a name, a drawing of the person, and their background.

"I did the sketches," Tisse declared, her small chest puffed out with pride. Mister Crawly Wawly, standing on her shoulder, looked pleased with himself, too.

The images were well-done. Tisse had a lot of special skills, from reviewing hot springs to writing books.

My mental image of an assassin had changed a lot because of her.

My sister's best friend was an interesting and charming individual.

"First, there's the Hero himself, Van of Flamberge." Rit pointed to the paper with the drawing of the boy possessed of a chivalrous, innocent expression. "He's the last surviving member of the Flamberge royal family. His country was destroyed by the demon lord's army. Van's place in the line of succession was low, and he left to study at a monastery in Avalonia at a young age. King Flamberge probably intended for his son to serve the church to strengthen his nation's connections with it. And thanks to that decision, Van was spared the flames of war."

"Raised in a monastery, huh? He sounds pretty out of touch with the outside world."

A monastery.

The church was a giant organization, but not immune to the ways of the world. Attempting to live strictly by divine law was difficult in reality, and no matter how faithful the cleric, there was always a need to strike a balance between divine mandate and mortal needs.

Claiming to tell the people the teachings of Demis merely by reading scripture at them wasn't helpful. Real support required knowing how people lived, understanding what they desired, and considering how to get through to them.

That way, the words of Demis became words for the people. That was how some clerics saw it anyway. And they were the ones who'd instituted monasteries.

A monastery was not open to normal students. It was a place removed from worldly temptations. A building where students weren't distanced from the divine for the sake of others.

Monasteries had been established as homes where one could exist solely for Demis.

Clerics who resided in monasteries were called monks, and they lived in them while contemplating only how to manifest divine law.

These days, so many years after the monasteries had been established, they were caught up in the church's internal power struggles like every other facet of the organization.

"Van's faith was nourished by growing up in a monastery. The members of the higher nobility in Flamberge believed that raising their children themselves was shameful. Their style was to entrust teaching and development to specialists," I said.

"Isn't that why there were so many feuds between members of the same family there?" Rit asked.

I shook my head. "I don't know. I never lived in Flamberge, and I can't claim to understand enough to criticize how things are done abroad."

"Well, I want to raise mine properly myself!"

"I'm in complete agreement."

"Heh-heh-heh…"

Rit concealed an embarrassed smile behind her red bandana.

Raised as a princess in the Duchy of Loggervia, she still had the habit of hiding her mouth whenever she grinned.

The way she does that is so cute.

"Ahem."

Yarandrala faked a cough.

Right, that derailed the conversation.

Rit's face reddened, and she returned to the subject of Van.

"…There's not a lot more we know about his past. He was sent to the monastery in Avalonia at a young age, and just a few months ago, during winter, he appeared at Last Wall fortress claiming he was the Hero."

"And that's where he met Cardinal Ljubo?"

"Yes. He was turned away at the gate, but he camped outside for days. After noticing that, Cardinal Ljubo summoned Van inside and spoke with him. At some point he recognized Van did have a genuine Hero blessing."

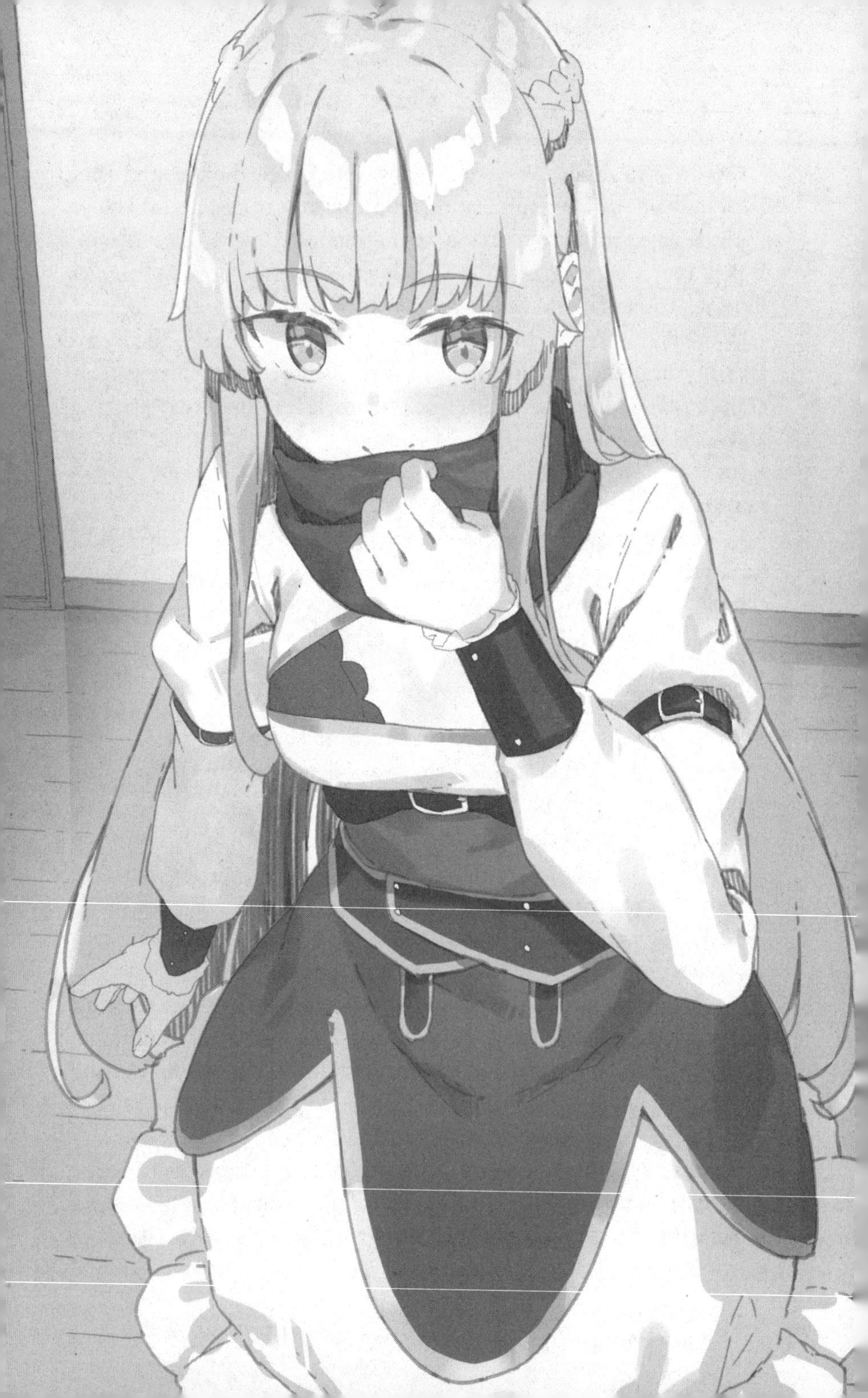

"Only those with a Cardinal blessing can become cardinals. But the Cardinal blessing doesn't have access to the Appraisal skill. Could he really be convinced of Van's blessing just by talking to him?"

Rit crossed her arms and considered my question.

"Before Ruti, it wasn't clear whether the Hero was fact or fiction, so maybe he decided to believe after comparing Van to her?"

"Hmmm..."

Ljubo definitely had a Saint with the Appraisal skill confirm it at some point. He didn't strike me as the sort to believe a boy claiming to be the Hero without any solid evidence.

"But after being recognized by the church, all he did was fight monsters and raise his level, yeah?" Danan asked as he read over the last bits of Van's background.

"He lost quite a few comrades in the process, too," I replied.

"Warriors of the church provided by Ljubo, probably. Guess he's used to party members dying now."

Yarandrala was mystified. "With the Hero blessing, shouldn't he be unable to abandon his comrades? So how did that many people die?"

"It's an issue of priority," I explained.

"Priority?"

"Yeah. Plenty of soldiers perished in battle while Ruti was there, but their deaths never slowed her down or left her incapable of going on."

"Now that you mention it..."

"The Hero's role is to save the world. If a person's death can be judged a necessary sacrifice, then there's no impulse to help that person. The world would never be saved if every soldier's passing caused the Hero to freeze up."

"But Van's party members died while they were hunting normal monsters."

"When battling normal monsters, Van apparently believes that his comrades' deaths are justified and necessary. The Hero's growth is more important than his comrades' lives. If he believes that from the depths of his heart, then it's conceivable that the Hero blessing allows him to abandon allies."

"I can't accept that!"

I laughed. The sound came out bitter. "The more you learn about blessings, the harder it becomes to accept a lot of things about them."

Blessings were the work of God. Even if they were unacceptable by the standards of mortals, divine law justified them...but we were people, not deities.

"Pissin' me off." Danan clenched his fist. The disgust on his face, as an angry vein swelled on his temple, would've been enough to knock out an average adventurer on the spot. "How can that guy be the Hero?!"

"Because that's what God decided. It's not that rare for a blessing's role and a person's attitude to clash."

"But this is the Hero, of all people!"

I was a bit surprised. Danan had previously claimed he'd only joined Ruti's party because he thought it was the quickest route to defeating the demon lord. However, it was clear from his voice that he had strong feelings about this topic.

"I understand how you feel, but calm down," Yarandrala chided. Still, it was clear she empathized. She vehemently rejected the Hero system that saddled one person with the fate of the world.

Tisse looked at me and smiled. "Ms. Ruti might not have seen us before the party broke up, but we saw her. The sight of her made us feel something. It's the only reason we continued the hopeless quest to defeat the demon lord and save the world."

"Right...," I said.

Ruti had hated the Hero blessing, but her travels hadn't been all bad. I hoped for her sake that there would come a day when that journey became a fond memory.

"That's all we have for Van. It's...not really much to go on." Rit looked a bit troubled. "When it comes to his thoughts, there's plenty to say, but regarding him as a person, he's pretty simple. Van's so straightforward there's not much to him."

"His world is small." Ruti's voice was cold. "Only Van and God exist in his world... No parents, no friends, no people he cares about."

"Small, huh?"

Ruti was right. However, that small world was also the source of Van's strength.

"His perception of things means he never doubts the values that form his faith. He never questions, never breaks. No matter what anyone else says or does, none in Van's world can damage his values."

Despite being pummeled by Ruti and left half-dead, Van had risen with a smile and declared that he would defeat Ruti. Worse yet, his only reason for doing so was to enhance his Hero blessing. It was logic predicated on pure faith without any rationality. None of us at the table were capable of the theological argumentation needed to beat such stubborn faith.

"Other than Theodora, we're all pretty disconnected from the church."

"Despite being members of the Hero's party."

That's why church officials didn't trust us and we'd had so much trouble during the fight at the Last Wall fortress, when Theodora had joined us.

"Knowing what we do about Van, I think our targets ought to be Ljubo and Lavender."

"No argument here."

Because of my Guide blessing, I had some thoughts on how Van was going about things, but this was not the time to bring them up.

It'd be a different story if the opportunity presented itself, but for now, it was best to focus on his party members.

"All right, Cardinal Ljubo and the fairy, Lavender."

The remaining two pieces of paper.

A smiling man in the prime of his life with a condescending gaze, and a beaming fairy with cold eyes.

"Unfortunately, we've got almost nothing for Lavender. She's a fairy who lived outside human society. Other than what Esta gave us, there's nothing. Not even a rumor."

"There's a limit to the information we can gather in Zoltan, after all. There aren't many travelers with news from beyond."

"I used the flying ship to investigate abroad, but all I could turn up about Lavender was that she's a fairy in Van's party and always clings to him," Tisse said.

Since Tisse could operate the airship, we'd asked her to gather intel outside Zoltan. Places that were weeks away by boat could be reached in a day on that vessel.

Ancient demon lord relics like the *Vendidad* and the airship had incredible capabilities.

I'd rather not give Van a flying ship.

"We know that Esta would prefer not to fight Lavender, and that's reason enough to consider her a top-tier archfay." Danan's tone was serious. "According to Esta, she fell in love with Van at first sight, betrayed her kin, and gave him a Behemoth Ring, a treasure of her secret woods."

"That's quite the extreme love." Rit had a pensive look on her face. "Why don't Danan and I try negotiating with her?"

"Me?"

Danan looked shocked.

"Is that a problem?"

"No. But I'm not much for diplomacy outside of making threats. It'll mostly be on you…"

Danan glanced at me, unsure of Rit's plan.

"I think leaving that to you two will be fine," I said.

"Really?"

"You're no good at negotiations, but Cardinal Ljubo will recognize you from the Last Wall fortress. So if Lavender decides to fight, I want you to protect Rit while you both retreat."

"Oh, bodyguard work? Okay, in that case, leave it to me!"

That was enough to make Danan accept it, and he grinned heartily.

"Do you have any reason to suspect talking with Lavender will be helpful?" Tisse asked. "We have no idea how she'll react."

Rit shook her head. "Success isn't the goal. The first objective will be to discern her motives. I don't believe she's doing all this entirely without reason."

"You think you can?"

"I'm in love myself, so I'm probably the one best equipped to understand her," Rit answered confidently, her cheeks getting a little red.

"Exactly. If any of us has a chance, it's Rit," I agreed. "So the next is Ljubo."

I picked up the remaining piece of paper.

"There's enough background on him that recounting it all would be a hassle. He has the Cardinal blessing. In terms of career, he followed the standard corrupt-inquisitor path to his current post."

"Just Ljubo? No last name?"

"So it would seem. He's from the western region of the Kingdom of Avalonia. Born to a family that raised horses."

"Not a pious or aristocratic upbringing."

"He apparently went to the church and built a reputation for himself solely off his Cardinal blessing. He used the bribes he collected as an inquisitor to reach his present position. Perhaps he turned to taking bribes because he lacked financial support from his family to fund his career."

Wicked ideals might have been the original reason he'd resorted to corruption, but...

"Whatever the reason, there's no mistaking his fondness for treasures and luxury," Yarandrala said.

From what I had gathered, his greed had shone through plenty of times during his tenure as a cardinal.

"His goal and his methods flipped somewhere along the line. The glitter of gold has that sort of magic to it," I remarked. And thus, a newly minted, avaricious man was born. "But that straightforwardness leaves plenty of openings, too." Greed was the easiest sort of motive to understand. "I'll speak with Ljubo."

"You?! But he'll recognize you!"

When we were adventuring, Ljubo had seen Ruti, Danan, and me when we fought at the Last Wall fortress. Tisse had accompanied him and the rest of Van's party on the quest to slay the hill giant Dundach. Plus, she was a part of Zoltan's only B-rank adventuring group. If Van or his comrades grew suspicious of her, they'd end up trying to track down her partner, Ruti. I preferred to keep Tisse out of this if possible.

"I have the Disguise skill. Ljubo doesn't have any ability to see through physical tricks, so it'll be fine."

"In that case, I'll go with you as backup." Yarandrala's voice was firm. Ljubo didn't know her. Although Yarandrala tended to be direct about her thoughts, she possessed enough negotiation experience to hide things when needed.

"All right. Rit and Danan will handle Lavender, and Yarandrala and I will deal with Ljubo. Ruti and Tisse will keep an eye out to intervene so we can safely escape if our discussions break down into a fight."

"Got it."

"No one's better at fleeing than an assassin. Leave it to me."

Mister Crawly Wawly hopped reassuringly.

"Has everyone memorized the info on these three? We have until they return from the south seas to prepare!" I said.

Everyone nodded. They were all reliable comrades.

I stood. "Okay. Now, how about some dinner?"

"I was waiting for that!"

Everyone laughed at Rit's cheerful response, and with that, our meeting concluded.

✻ ✻ ✻

The following day, I visited Ruti's plantation.

"Welcome, Big Brother."

Ruti greeted me with a happy look.

Actually, she'd come by my place for breakfast and walked to her farm with me…but when the plots came into view, she'd rushed ahead so she could pop out and greet me.

So cute.

"You were up late last night making medicine, right? If you tell me what you need and how much, I can gather it."

"Sounds good. Guess I'll leave that work to you today."

"Mhm."

Ruti's voice was firm, and she clenched her fists.

I had enough training that one night without sleep wasn't a big deal, but there was no need to force myself to do everything alone like I used to. I handed Ruti a note listing the herbs I needed.

"Understood."

After a little salute, Ruti headed to the fields in high spirits with tools in hand. The way she looked in her plain clothes suited to fieldwork, the sort a normal village girl might wear, made for a peaceful scene. There was no better sight.

I have to protect this.

"Red."

Turning around, I saw Tisse holding a steaming cup.

"This might take a little while, so let's wait inside."

The two of us went inside the shed beside the plots. The office had more things in it than the last time I'd come by.

"We've had more purchase orders for herbs than just those from your shop."

Ruti's name had spread around Zoltan after the incident with Veronia. Her plantation still lacked a proven track record, but her name was enough to get a few people interested in doing business.

"However, with only Ms. Ruti and me running the plantation, we can't take that many orders."

"If you hire some people, you could expand."

"No. Ms. Ruti and I discussed that at the start, and we're not interested in making this a large business. We want to enjoy life."

Tisse sipped her black tea with a tranquil smile.

I tried some as well. The mixed-in apple jam went well with the tea, creating a pleasant taste.

"I have prepared everything I can at the moment," Tisse stated abruptly. She was referring to the Van situation. "But…ultimately, I am still an assassin. I don't have confidence in my ability to resolve problems in ways beyond killing. I regularly think, 'Is this really okay?' 'Is there nothing else I can do before Hero Van returns?' And so on."

"Ah. So you feel uneasy sitting here and relaxing."

"Yes."

It was for a short while, but Tisse had accompanied Van and his companions and seen them fight.

"Van the Hero felt more scary than strong. My Assassin blessing told me he'd be difficult to kill. The feeling was greater than when I met Danan and Theodora."

"Coming from the world's strongest assassin, that certainly has weight. So his power is at least enough for him to aspire to save the world."

"You crossed blades with him as well, right? What did you feel?"

I touched the hilt of the bronze sword at my waist.

My battle with Van had only been about stalling for time until Ruti arrived. I'd never intended to defeat him, and I'd known he didn't mean to retreat. I'd leveraged the advantages I had to survive.

"Hmm, it was unmistakably the fighting style unique to the Hero... His idea of the Hero was very different from Ruti's."

"'Idea'?"

"The Hero is a blessing with a wealth of skills to choose from. You can understand the sort of Hero someone aims to be by how they fight and the skills they take."

In Ruti's case, I'd given her advice on developing her abilities, so her ideas of the Hero included some of my own. Hers was a Hero that didn't lose. No matter how terrifying the opponent, be it a superior warrior, countless armies, giant monsters, malicious conspiracies, invisible plagues and curses, or natural disasters...the Hero who was compelled to save everyone had to handle every kind of obstacle.

The Hero was undoubtedly the strongest Divine Blessing, but there were still bound to be fights Ruti couldn't win. That's why I'd suggested a Hero that didn't lose. So that even if she couldn't emerge victorious, that setback would never be the end.

"By the time I knew her, she was already stronger than everyone, but she didn't get that way alone."

"Honestly, even without her blessing, my little sister is a genius when it comes to sword fighting."

"I think that's probably because you taught her."

"Because of me?"

Tisse giggled.

"People are more enthusiastic when they're instructed by people important to them."

"Ahh. That's true."

A good connection with your master was important.

"So then, from your perspective, what is Van's idea of the Hero?"

"One without enemies."

"Without enemies?!" Tisse's eyes widened. Given how skilled she was at hiding her emotions, this had to be a considerable shock.

"There are no enemies for Van's Hero."

"Coming from you, that's…"

"Er, well, I don't mean it exactly like that."

That was a bad way to put it.

"Van's determined to become a Hero who will always win. He has a skill set optimized for endurance, and his Healing Hands mastery can push his damage on others. It's a powerful combination. But it's a build that doesn't factor in the opponent. It's an ideal that envisions simply winning with the strongest possible attack regardless of what his foes do."

"Ah…I understand. You mean his sword has no thought except the confidence that he will triumph so long as he can use his best attack."

While Ruti had considered every possible enemy in the process of making sure she'd never lose, Van sought the strength to win against every opponent with the same technique.

At a glance, the two methods were similar, but the approaches were opposites.

"That style is popular among people with high-tier blessings or those specialized in specific directions. I understand why someone with the strongest blessing chose that route. It's not how I'd go about it, though."

"Nor I. Observation is critical in my old line of work. An assassin's blade is capable of incredible things, but anyone who relies solely on it will know defeat someday. I see."

Van's world was small. And that shaped the ideal Hero he strove to be.

"I don't know if Van will be able to survive fighting the demon lord's armies. Right now, he stands no chance against Ruti. If defeating him were all it took to resolve this, we'd have nothing to worry about."

"Van's relying on the strength of his blessing, but Ms. Ruti is a more powerful Hero."

"Yeah."

That's why I remained so calm despite knowing Van aimed to kill Ruti.

"Unfortunately, Ruti's might can't break Van's spirit. Because there is no enemy for his sword."

"He doesn't understand that he can't win."

"I wonder if that's also part of his blessing…the courage to keep fighting without end, even when it's hopeless."

"Shouldn't the Hero search for a way to defeat such a superior opponent?"

I shrugged. "Anyway, that's the gist of what I gleaned while fighting him. Did that help you any?"

"Yes… I feel like I understand what was so frightening about Van. Admittedly, I still can't put it into words, though."

"Our opponent has the Divine Blessing of the Hero. He's different from every other challenge we've faced."

I smiled to put Tisse at ease.

"But right now, we're acting to avoid fighting him. It would be a waste to get too cautious and forget about the day-to-day right in front of us."

The door opened with a creak.

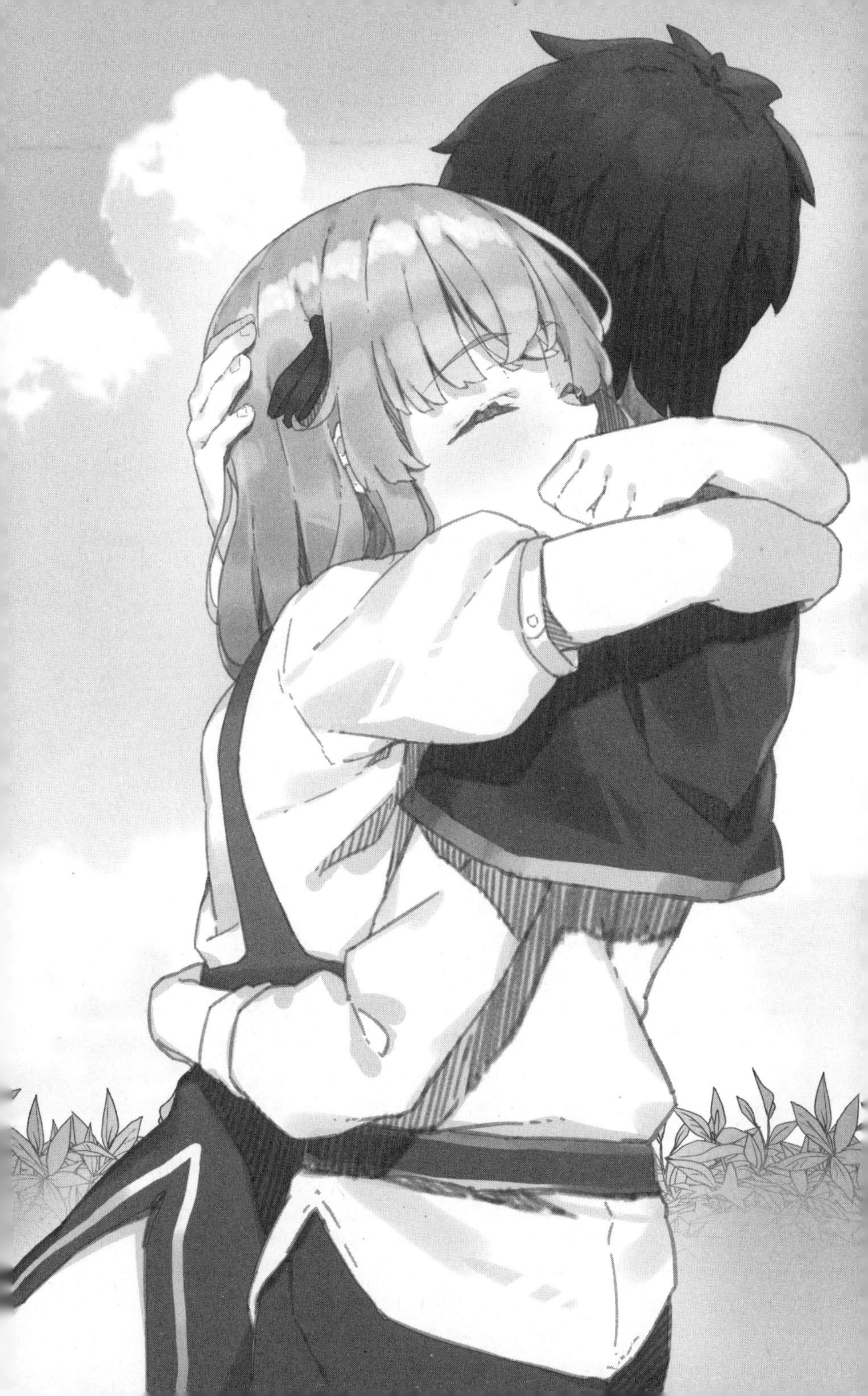

"I've gathered the herbs, Big Brother."

"Good work. Can I see?"

"Mhm. Here you go."

The basket Ruti held out contained the different things I'd requested, all neatly packed away. It was clear at a glance how much of each particular plant was bundled.

That's my Ruti.

"Thank you. That's everything I asked for."

"Mhm."

Ruti smiled proudly.

Adorable.

"That will cover the store's inventory. Given the current situation, I wanted to avoid going to the mountains."

"Was I helpful, Big Brother?"

"Of course. Thanks, Ruti."

"Heh-heh."

Seeing Ruti's happy expression made me glad as well.

When I patted her head, Ruti wrapped me in a hug.

"Today is a good day," she said, despite it still being early.

✸ ✸ ✸

Once I got back to the shop, I set to work preparing medicine and left tending the counter to Rit.

"That's enough for the medicinal cookies. So I can skim off the top layer from the boiling herbs and blend it with this paste…"

I didn't have a skill to speed up preparation.

For me, it was all about making the most efficient use of time.

Turning over the hourglasses on the table, having herbs boiling and steaming while simultaneously crushing and blending other ingredients.

Grinding plants to make a paste, forming a solution by boiling them in water, creating an extract by steaming them. Herbs had many uses.

"I need to add some more wood to strengthen the flames. Ah, the charring on this pot has gotten bad. I'll need to get it fixed up soon."

I took the flask of extract from its holder and cooled it in a bucket of water.

"It's been a while since I was this busy with work."

Back when I was a knight, there were times when operations were coordinated by the second.

"I guess a little hustle isn't so bad occasionally."

It was a pleasant interruption to an otherwise slow-paced life.

"Sure is hot, though…"

Perhaps that was to be expected when I was working in a cramped space with a fire going.

I had a cloth covering my face to keep sweat from mixing into the concoctions, which only made it stuffier.

"It really feels like I'm working hard."

That odd sense of satisfaction kept me feeling good while I took the pot off the flame.

The next step could wait until the contents cooled naturally.

"Time for a break… Whoops, looks like I'm a bit late on lunch."

I stood and stretched, groaning as I worked out the kinks.

"Good work!" Rit's voice rang out. "Ready for lunch? I made food, so come have some!"

"You made lunch?"

"Yep!"

After washing my hands, I went into the living room and saw the dishes Rit had made lined up on the table. Sausage and sunny-side-up eggs, sautéed tomatoes and mushrooms, tomato-simmered broad beans, bread and jam, and a lettuce and cheese salad.

For dessert, there were cherries and apples.

"It looks great."

"Unlike you, I can only manage simple cooking, but the feelings I put into it are just as strong!"

"That you made so much is plenty. Let's dig in."

"Yeah!"

Rit's cooking was simple. The more manipulation you did, the more influence cooking skills had, so less complex dishes tended to be tastier.

I'd made the jam and salad dressing, and the sauce for the tomato-simmered beans was one I'd used to flavor the soup I'd made that morning. The bread came from a local baker. The dessert was just cut fruits, meaning a cooking skill wouldn't have affected the flavor. The eggs, sausage, and sautéed tomatoes and mushrooms had all been cooked and salted for taste.

I had a bite.

"Delicious."

As expected of Rit. She clearly understood the limits of food preparation without a relevant skill and chose the best dishes she could.

I could tell from the simple and marvelous food just how much thought she'd put into making something I'd enjoy. Just like she'd said, this meal was imbued with her feelings. That was what made it great.

* * *

"Here's the plate."

"Thanks!"

Clink.

Rit and I stood shoulder to shoulder doing the dishes.

I used a brush made from palm fibers to wash while Rit wiped with a dishrag and then put the dinnerware back on the shelf.

Everything had been set in a bucket of water to make it easier to clean, and the stack was quickly shrinking.

"Here's the last one."

"Since it's the last, I'll do an extra-good job on the drying!"

The plate squeaked in Rit's hands as she wiped it down.

"Okay, perfect!"

Rit beamed, and naturally, I did, too.

"Good work, Rit."

"Good work, Red."

We high-fived with both hands once we finished, then hugged and kissed each other on the cheek before returning to apothecary responsibilities.

I returned to the workroom.

"Hmm-hmm."

I started humming to myself, a clear indication of my good mood.

"Should I make powdered titan crab shell and scorching stone powder?"

Both were rare ingredients, but only a few grams of each was needed to make a single dose of medicine.

Keeping the ingredients in storage and breaking off just a fingernail-size portion to crush when necessary was more than enough. However, if there was time to spare, there was no problem with grinding up a little now.

I stored the powder I made in a bottle and set it on the shelf.

Then I mixed the solution that had boiled in the meantime with another herb and added some honey to make a pill.

And finally, I divided up the medicines.

"Phew. That's all of the reserves taken care of."

I gave myself a pat on the back as I examined the tightly packed shelves.

Peering out the window, I saw it was already evening.

"I just made it by closing time. Maybe I should check on Rit."

After changing out of my dirty clothes, I headed to the storefront.

"Thanks for the purchase!"

I was just in time to see Rit say good-bye to a customer.

There were still two others picking out what they wanted.

"Red! Finished making everything?"

"Yeah, just now."

"Great! Good job!"

Rit's shoulders tensed a bit.

She really wanted to hug me, but held back because of the customers. I understood that only because I felt the same desire.

"Eh-heh-heh, it's about thirty minutes until closing time. What are you going to do? You can take a break if you want."

"No, I'll keep you company."

"Heh-heh. Okay."

I stood next to Rit.

The two of us managed the counter together. We counted money, packed orders and handed them to customers, and explained various medicines' effects.

A break would've been nice, too, but I enjoyed working together with Rit.

Any moment spent with Rit was a content one.

""Thanks for the purchase!""

Closing time.

We saw off the last patron, an adventurer who'd come to get medicine for a quest tomorrow. She thanked us with evident relief. "I don't know what I would have done without this."

"We sold lots of medicine! And ran out of cookies again! Yep, it really feels like a good day's work!"

"We haven't developed any new products, but our clientele is still increasing."

"Our apothecary's reputation has gone up. Isn't that great?"

"Yeah, it's nice that more people know our shop."

The simple apothecaries Red and Rit had found a home in Zoltan and were able to enjoy a happy life.

"All right, shall we close?"

"Yeah!"

I left the counter to Rit and headed outside with a broom.

I hung the C<small>LOSED</small> sign on the door.

"There we go."

When I looked up, I saw the sign above the entrance with R<small>ED</small> & R<small>IT</small>'s A<small>POTHECARY</small> written on it.

"Hmm…"

I returned to the store.

"Something up?" Rit cocked her head.

"No, I just felt like cleaning up the sign out front a bit."

I took a towel and bucket from the washroom and took the ladder from the closet before heading outside again.

First, I wiped the sign down with a dry towel to remove the dust.

"Somewhere along the way, this dirt gave it all a bit of gravitas."

The fresh, new sign had gotten messy while hanging out front, but that signified everything the shop had been through. I felt a little melancholy for dusting it off.

When I finished, I wet the towel in the bucket of water and started washing.

Once the sign was clean again, I noticed it had a different feel from when it was new.

After climbing off the ladder, I suddenly found myself thinking that we were lucky to have had such a good sign made for us.

*   *   *

That night, I locked the storefront and turned around.

"I'll be back soon, Rit."

"Okay, take care. I'll be back soon, too."

"Yeah, take care."

We chuckled a bit in the moonlight before parting.

I was going to gather information for my talk with Cardinal Ljubo, and Rit was doing the same for her talk with Lavender.

How would she sway Lavender when we hardly knew anything about her…? I couldn't begin to guess. That was why I'd entrusted it to Rit, I suppose.

I had to focus on the things I could do.

My destination was the church in central Zoltan.

A voice replied, "Right on schedule" after I used the door knocker.

Unhurried footfalls approached.

When the door opened, I saw Bishop Shien wearing comfortable clothes. A smile crossed his wrinkled face.

"Zoltan people are casual when it comes to time, so it's surprising to get such a prompt visit."

"Hah-hah. Aren't you from Zoltan?"

"I studied at the church in Central. Anyone who dared to sleep in would get a terrible scolding from the deacon in charge."

"It must have been rough when you were at the bottom rungs."

"You seem like you've had your share of difficult work when you were at the bottom rungs, too."

Whoops.

"Hah-hah. Don't worry. I'm not trying to pry." Bishop Shien grinned. "Now then, it seems the hot water has come to a boil while we were chatting. The truth is, you were so on time I didn't have the tea ready."

"Sounds great. It was warm today, but it's still a bit chilly at night."

I stepped inside, and Bishop Shien led me to his quarters. I took a seat across from him.

"Now then, it seems you have something you wanted to ask me."

"It's about Cardinal Ljubo."

His expression grew serious, and he nodded. "I suspected as much."

"I heard that you spoke with Cardinal Ljubo when you went to negotiate to keep the church from intervening in the conflict with Veronia."

"Indeed. His Eminence was among those pushing for war and had backed a military intervention. It was necessary that I convince him to abstain."

"How was he?"

"Hmmm… I am just a simple country bishop, and it has been a long time since I left Central for Zoltan, so I don't have much confidence in my eye for people. But if my impressions are enough for you…"

"I'd like to hear your thoughts."

"I got the impression Cardinal Ljubo was a *reasonable* man."

That same sort of description again...

"When I heard he was in favor of intervention, I was suspicious, expecting fierce opposition... Yet upon my meeting him, Cardinal Ljubo had a smile and received me quite reasonably."

"Do you think he is a good cleric?"

"I believe he is keenly attuned to his interests."

He'd probably recognized how unfavorable it was to continue pushing for war and so pulled back. Did that mean I ought to try convincing him that remaining in Zoltan was wasteful?

"However..."

When he saw me slip into contemplation, Bishop Shien's gaze sharpened. His eyes were those of an adventurer more than those of a priest.

"The deacon who taught me warned me that Cardinal Ljubo is not to be trusted."

"'Not to be trusted...'?"

"Yes. He is not the sort who hesitates to betray. There are no public records of it, but apparently, he accused the priest who'd been like a father to him of heresy and had him executed."

"It's hard to believe there's no surviving account of that."

"It was for a cardinal—surely a piece of some internal power struggle."

"So Ljubo chose someone useful over someone who took care of him?"

This cardinal was a dangerous man. Perhaps that befitted one of Van the Hero's comrades.

Someone who felt little in the way of obligation or empathy might not respect promises, either. He likely wouldn't care much about any damage that befell Zoltan so long as it helped Van. I'd need to limit myself to Ljubo's personal costs and benefits when dealing with him.

Honestly, that sounded like a challenge, but it would be easier than trying to sway Van himself.

* * *

Three days later, Ruti and I left Rit to close the shop in the evening and headed to a field away from the main road. Once sure we were out of sight, Ruti summoned a spirit mount for us to ride.

"It's been a while."

"This is a first for me."

We rode through a glade and into the forest.

Suddenly, a fog appeared, but as we pressed forward, I heard the sound of a brook.

"Things were a bit different the last time I was here. Let's try following the sound."

"Understood."

Ruti pulled the reins and changed direction as we proceeded through the woods.

After a little while, the mist cleared, and we reached a collection of mushroom houses.

"A fairy village."

Ruti looked around.

Rit and I had visited this place once.

"I get to see it with Big Brother."

Ruti seemed pleased.

"Red!"

The fay gathered around me.

"Nice to see you!"

"It's been a while."

"'Been a while'?"

The fairies cocked their heads and then started laughing as if I'd said something funny.

"Hee-hee, the flow of time means little to us, so a few minutes or a few hundred years are much the same."

A beautiful woman with a body of translucent water greeted us. Her bare body was a perfect beauty, the sort typically found only in paintings.

"Welcome to my humble pool!"

This was Undine, archfay of water.

The fairies, who were previously cursed, now looked healthy and cheerful.

※　　　　　　※　　　　　　※

"Here's the item you requested."

"Thank you. I appreciate it." I received the leather bag.

"Not at all. You are our benefactor and friend. You may ask for such presents whenever you desire," Undine said with a smile.

In truth, I should have prepared something as thanks, and the fact I hadn't been able to bothered me a bit.

Once this thing with Van is settled, maybe I'll come back with something.

While I thought it over, Ruti looked all around.

"What's happening?" Ruti asked Undine.

"Nothing. This is just preparation to ensure the water will remain the same brook it was the day before."

"Because of the Hero? Or the fairy?"

Undine put her hand to her mouth, surprised by Ruti's inquiry.

"You are quite perceptive. The fairy."

"Lavender, huh?"

"That is apparently what she is calling herself."

Undine's expression turned serious.

If Lavender can make an archfay look like that...

"She is a truly terrifying being who must be avoided."

"Unfortunately, we don't have that luxury. We're trying to get her and the others to leave Zoltan."

"I see. In that case, you must not let your guard down around her. There is no other fairy so fickle or loving of destruction."

Undine had always looked cheerful, even when weakened by a curse. For her to look so intense now meant Lavender was truly a grave threat.

"That aside—" Undine's cheerful smile returned in the blink of an eye, "—since Red's little sister has come to visit, we have to make sure she enjoys herself before leaving!"

The fairies fluttered around Ruti.

"Do you want tea and cookies?"

"Or do you want to dance with us?"

"No way, you should take a stroll with us!"

Ruti was a little surprised by the pushy creatures.

She smiled and took my hand. "You should play with us, too."

After enjoying ourselves in the fairy village, we secretly hopped the wall back into Zoltan in the dark.

Is Rit going to be annoyed?

"Big Brother, today was a good day."

Ruti was happy, so I figured it was okay.

* * *

Another three days later, we were in the backyard at night.

"Are you ready, Brother?"

"Yeah, ready when you are."

I held up my bronze sword.

Ruti stood across from me with a stick.

The branch was about the length of Ruti's sword and of its replica that Van wielded.

I was about to start combat training with Ruti.

"Here I go."

Ruti slowly raised the stick into a middle stance. Tremendous pressure emanated from her. This was the strongest girl in the world.

Ordinarily, no one would dare dream of facing such overwhelming force.

"Hah."

Ruti disappeared after a single breath.

"Yah!"

She merely charged straight at me and swiped with the stick, yet she did so with such speed that my eyes couldn't keep up.

Clack!

My sword deflected her attack.

I couldn't see the incoming strike, but I knew the timing it would land with.

"That's my big brother. I'm going to keep coming."

The stick flashed.

Clack! Clack! Clack! Clack! The sound of metal against wood rang out countless times.

I was able to parry because Ruti was using a stick. Were it a holy sword, my blade would be long since shattered.

I suppose a bronze sword does have its limits...

"Hyah!"

"There!"

Dodging Ruti's swipe at my neck, I pressed my sword against her stick the moment it reached the end of its arc.

However, no sooner did our weapons meet than Ruti's arm vanished. A blink later, the stick was pressed against my neck.

"I give up."

I relaxed and surrendered.

"Hahhhh."

After I caught my breath, my muscles were crying in agony.

"That stings..."

So by using a magic potion to raise my reflexes and strength while also employing the special breathing method I learned as a knight, I can just barely manage to keep up...

"Are you okay?"

Ruti's hand shone gently as she touched me.

Healing Hands immediately restored the damaged muscles.

"Thanks, Ruti."

"You're welcome."

I used every possible trick I could and only barely managed... Ruti's strong.

"Amazing!"

Rit rushed over with a towel in hand.

"No one else could take that much while fighting Ruti."

"It isn't an actual battle, though."

The training was just Ruti attacking with a stick and me defending. She wasn't allowed to do anything but strike, limiting the patterns of her actions.

"Had she wielded a sword, my blade would have broken."

I held the bronze sword up in the moonlight. There were nicks on the blade from where it had met the stick.

"Leftovers from when I couldn't deflect and had to simply block."

Parrying and guarding had different timing. When facing an opponent with a strong weapon with a fragile one of your own, like a bronze sword, it was crucial to deflect the force of incoming blows without catching too much of the power on the blade itself. By parrying with perfect timing, Ruti could defend against even a giant's blow with that wooden stick.

"But...*he's* not an opponent to intentionally fight with a weak weapon."

I'd originally used a bronze sword, because it was my little way of resisting the memories of all that time I'd spent fighting. My old life had left me unable to sleep without a weapon in reach, even though I wanted to live peacefully.

Since Ruti had been freed from the Hero blessing's impulses, I'd managed to get my mind in order, and now I slept just fine without a sword at hand. I kept using a bronze sword because there was no reason to buy a more expensive one, and I'd grown attached to the weapon.

However, a bronze sword wouldn't be very reliable when I was going up against the Hero and his comrades.

"Well, we don't intend to fight for the moment."

"But there's no harm in being ready for it. Right?"

"Right."

That was the point of training with Ruti.

I was practicing my defense to ensure a safe retreat if a battle with Van the Hero became inevitable.

"All right, Ruti, again, please."

"Got it."

I'd used what was an expensive magic potion to me these days for this training.

I ought to get the most out of it before the effects wear off.

Practice with Ruti continued for another hour.

Even with my Immunity to Fatigue, an hour of dealing with Ruti's attacks was enough to wear down my body and spirit. Had it been anyone but Ruti, I would've started complaining by now.

By the time it was finally over, I was dead tired. However...

"My turn!"

Rit stood ready, barehanded instead of holding a weapon.

Pushing yourself when exhausted was how you reached a breakthrough and climbed to a new level. That was the excuse I gave myself anyway. Honestly, I just wanted to train with Rit, too, since I'd practiced with Ruti.

"All right, I'll try a three-attack combo that begins with a high kick. The movements will be improvised after the opener."

"Okay."

The training with Rit involved combinations in which she announced her opening strike. The practice was meant to test both our offensive and our defensive techniques.

"Go for it, Big Brother."

Ruti tied a handkerchief to her stick and waved it like a flag to cheer me on while she sipped apple juice.

"Hah!"

Rit's leg flew upward.

It was a high kick from a distance.

I leaped back to dodge it, and she spun her body to loose a second kick.

With both her legs in the air, she planted her hands on the ground to pivot and unleash a kick down at me from above for the third attack.

It was a beautiful maneuver, enough to take my breath away even though I was on the defensive.

Perhaps because Rit used two swords, kicks were her bread and butter for unarmed fighting.

Rit's kicks were strong enough to break an average warrior's neck, but this was training, so she didn't put all her strength into each blow.

However, I didn't have any skills for fighting without a weapon. If I blocked one of her strikes, I could end up with my arms broken. So I did my best to evade incoming attacks.

"A high-low combo followed by a roundhouse!"

Rit continued unleashing different strikes.

I defended in response, but hand-to-hand fighting was something I only practiced on the side. I couldn't stop everything and took more than a few hits for it.

"Not quite!"

"Ah!"

While taking a kick, I seized Rit's leg the moment it stopped moving.

The fighting style was different, but the breathing techniques of swordsmanship were still effective.

Rit tried to get her leg free, but before she could, I swept her other one out from under her.

Her stance broke immediately.

"Hup."

I made sure to catch her before she hit the ground.

"Heh-heh-heh. That's my Red."

"I took a couple hits, though. In a real fight, my movements would have dulled from the damage. This one's your win."

"Hmm. Maybe. Well, there's no winners or losers in training."

"True."

The two of us chuckled.

It was more like we were working out together than fighting.

A competition without any intent to actually beat the opponent was interesting in its own way when compared to standard battle.

"I want to try, too," said Ruti.

"Okay. We can take turns so everyone gets a shot," I replied

"Our match was completely one-sided at the colosseum in Loggervia, but I should have a chance in a bout of unarmed techniques!" Rit declared

"Big Brother taught me how to fight...with extreme attention to detail. So I won't lose in this kind of battle, either."

Rit and Ruti were getting fired up.

I had confidence with a sword, but far less with my fists. That Ruti boasted about my training her in weaponless fighting was a bit troubling.

Regardless, she and Rit clearly enjoyed sparring with each other.

Such a thing would've been impossible for the old Ruti.

Even when her attacks weren't intended to defeat an opponent outright, she still had the overwhelming might of the Hero.

She could call upon that intense pressure when necessary, of course, but these days she was able to keep it in check and practice forms and stances with people besides me.

Seeing how much fun it was for her reinforced my commitment to protecting our life here.

I'm not gonna let some new Hero disrupt things.

"Next is me and Ruti," I said.

"Mhm. A step in, middle kick aimed at the chin, a spear hand aimed at the neck, three strikes to center mass, leg sweep, and follow-up attack when you fall."

"O-okay. Whenever you're ready."

I'd taught her some hand-to-hand fighting, but I didn't recall that combination.

It's probably best that I don't face the Hero without a weapon...

※   ※   ※

Late that night, after the special training concluded and Ruti left, hot water from the tub overflowed and spilled onto the floor.

"*Ahhhh.*"

Rit and I groaned with delight.

"The water feels great." Rit's voice was relaxed.

I agreed completely. "A bath after a good workout is sublime."

"I wonder if our muscles are going to be sore tomorrow."

"I had some good exercise recently from that sparring match with Danan, so I'll probably be okay."

"What a shame. I was going to suggest we massage each other."

Rit giggled and took my hand.

It'd become normal for us to bathe together.

"Rub rub." Rit started massaging my hand. "I'll have to settle for just this, I suppose."

"I-it's just a massage. We can just do that whenever we like, can't we? It feels nice even if I don't have muscle aches."

Why'd I have to open my big mouth?

"Heh-heh-heh." Rit's face reddened a bit as she smiled happily. "True. Shall we have a massage match when we get out of the bath?"

I'm sure it was just the water that made my face feel so warm.

"Y-yeah." My response came out weaker than I'd intended. I needed more training. "So should we call this practice, too?"

Rit burst out laughing.

"I don't think there's any part of you I haven't touched or vice versa…" I was losing my composure more and more as she spoke. And she was enjoying seeing me shaken.

Is she getting flushed because of the bath?

"You're the only one. The only man who has touched me here," Rit said as she held up her big, soft breasts. And then an impish grin flashed across her face.

"But I don't know if I've touched here yet."

"Ahh?!"

I poked a spot on her breast with my finger.

Rit shuddered.

At least I can do this much without too much trouble!

"Mrgh! You touched there just the other day!" Rit wrapped her arms around me.

Water splashed out of the tub.

"I don't know if I've touched you here before, though." Rit kissed an old scar on my neck.

"Don't you touch that every day?"

"Heh-heh. I like that part of you."

There were more splashes.

Even in the warm bath, Rit's skin against mine was still hotter than anything.

I held her tight, and she looked into my eyes. Her soft lips met mine.

"I love you."

Rit was beautiful as she said that. I smiled gently, face red.

*　　*　　*

The bedroom.

I was holding Rit while looking at the moon through the window.

"It sure is beautiful tonight."

Rit closed her eyes. I gently massaged her slightly sweaty shoulders.

"Heh-heh." She giggled, but kept her eyes closed.

This was a moment of irreplaceable happiness.

"...They'll be back soon, won't they?"

Rit opened her eyes.

Van and his party.

The sleepiness evaporated from Rit's face.

I took a deep breath and focused my drifting mind.

"He's raising his blessing level. I don't know how high he'll get before he's satisfied, but going on what Theodora said, he should be back soon."

"We've done all we can, haven't we?"

"Yeah. We have."

We were only capable of so much, but we'd done our best to prepare.

"Let's give it our best shot."

"Yeah."

Why were we fighting against the Hero and the church, against the embodiments of what was right?

After today, I knew exactly why.

Even if our opponent was a blessing meant to save the world, I refused to waver.

Our happiness was far more precious than the Hero.

Rit and I held each other and fell into peaceful sleep.

And the Hero returned to Zoltan.

Chapter 2

Targeting the Fairy in Love and the Greedy Cardinal

Zoltan's harbor was situated a little beyond the river mouth, enough so that the demon lord's ship couldn't reach it.

Van the Hero landed in Zoltan's harbor on a yacht lowered from the *Vendidad*.

"Is it okay to keep the crew on the ship?" Van asked as he leaped onto the pier.

"Sailors are cowards who will run the moment they touch dry land. A key point when sailing the seas is not letting them off the ship if possible." Ljubo spoke sagaciously, but his face was pale from seasickness.

"It's unwise to let them off all at once, but it's common to let them disembark in rotating shifts." The masked warrior Esta looked tired as she stepped onto the pier.

"I'll take care of the luggage."

Esta's squire, Albert, dexterously used his prosthetic right hand to unload the party's belongings from the boat.

A small figure watched lazily from her perch on Van's shoulder.

"…Hmph."

"Hmm? What is it?"

"Humans are unreliable creatures… Except for you, of course, Van!"

Lavender kissed his cheek.

Van the Hero's party had returned.

"The south seas made for a good trip. Not a lot of people go there, so there were many monsters with high blessing levels." Van beamed with satisfaction.

There were no scars since he'd restored himself completely with Healing Hands, but his armor showed signs of damage. It would need to be repaired.

"I'm definitely stronger now. I want to see if my strength is enough to vanquish the Hero's enemy right away!"

"You'll win for sure next time! Since I'll be fighting with you!"

Van and Lavender were getting excited. However, Esta, Albert, and Ljubo wore grave expressions.

"Cardinal Ljubo." Esta's voice was cold. "Is there any reason to endanger the Hero here?"

"…A warrior out here in the middle of nowhere is surely nothing to him."

"Do you truly believe that? You saw it yourself, didn't you? He was on the verge of death. Do you think you or I could manage that?"

"Hmph. Indeed. It is concerning. But it is still impossible to accept that such a mighty warrior lives in this backwater."

"There is no denying that Van was utterly trounced."

"Esta, this is an order as your employer."

"Sir."

"Look into the identity of the girl who defeated Van. I will restrain the boy until you learn more."

"Gathering information is not my forte, and there's little I can do without knowing what she looks like…but I suppose I'm the best one for the job in this party. Understood. Albert and I will look into it."

"As soon as you can."

This is fortunate, at least. Van's less likely to suddenly attack Ruti now. I just have to find an opening to meet with the others, thought Esta. She knew nothing she said could stop Van anymore. *It's pathetic, but I have to rely on them.*

Her eyes dropped as she scoffed at herself behind the mask. The self-derision lasted only a moment, though. By the next second, she was looking straight ahead and pushing forward.

✳   ✳   ✳

Hmmm…

I was disguised as a roadside merchant on the outskirts of the harbor, observing Van and the others.

Van's blessing had increased by thirteen levels since he'd fought me.

It was an impossible rate of growth for such a short time. Undoubtedly, he'd fought monsters day and night the whole time he was gone, pushing himself to the brink.

I suppose that means I can chalk the gloomy mood coming from the Vendidad *up to crew casualties.*

Van wasn't the first to treat his sailors poorly, but I wondered how morale would hold up when it came time for him to sail that vessel around the world to fight the demon lord's army.

It wasn't my responsibility to fret over, though. I had to focus on that excitable fairy on Van's shoulder.

Tisse was watching from a location on the other side of the harbor, and Lavender's focus shifted in that direction. The fairy had detected a world-class assassin, a feat even higher-level demons couldn't manage.

Nothing had suggested Lavender was especially wary of Tisse before. If she had been, she would've reacted in some way when Tisse joined Van's group to clear out the hill giants.

Perhaps she was able to see through Tisse's stealth because she'd met her before. Lavender might have memorized some quality unknown to humans and be able to sense it within a certain range.

What a troublesome ability.

The real issue was the range. Tisse was around three hundred meters from Van's party. I guessed it had been optimistic to assume that was enough distance. It was best to assume Lavender possessed some incredibly long-range sensory ability, much like the archfay Undine, who had been able to detect me moving through the river.

Lavender might also be curious about Esta and Albert's whereabouts, so it was better not to let Tisse convene with them.

So…what kind of fairy is she?

I wasn't a specialist when it came to the fay, but I knew at least a little about most varieties from studying books. There were lots of things about fairies that remained a mystery to humans, so I couldn't profess to know every subset. Still, there was something uncanny about Lavender that differentiated her from every other fay I'd encountered.

She looked like just a standard pixie, but that was a facade. My gut told me that that wasn't her true form.

"Will Rit be okay?"

I felt a little worried about Lavender learning of Rit's existence.

* * *

On the evening of the next day, Rit and Danan walked down a road on the outskirts of Zoltan, each of them wearing a cloak with a deep hood.

They didn't attempt to hide their movements, yet no one noticed them.

They walked without sound and presence. Should a normal person have looked upon them, they wouldn't have noticed anything there. The only nearby person who managed to catch them was Galatine, a higher-up in the Adventurers Guild who happened to be enjoying steak at a café along the road.

Seeing Rit, he stopped eating for a moment. But after a moment's consideration, he chose to return to his meal. He decided there was no way that Rit of all people would do this without good reason, and that it likely concerned the Van problem causing a stir in town. It was best to leave her to it rather than act unknowingly and disrupt the plan.

Galatine trusted Rit and her comrades enough to entrust them with Zoltan's future.

"I'll have some wine, please."

"Sure thing."

A cheerful waitress brought out a bottle of red.

Galatine chose to forget about the two figures he'd spied until he was needed, content to listen to the wine pouring into the glass.

Rit and Danan entered an alley.

"Sneaking all around us, masking your presences. Are you trying to tick me off?"

A small fairy waited for them there with her arms crossed.

Danan whistled. "Went just like you said it would."

"That's how it goes with people who are confident in their strength."

Rit smirked from within her deep hood.

Separating Lavender from Van had proven a challenging obstacle to overcome. However, Rit had taken advantage of Lavender's scorn for most humans.

How would someone react upon realizing people were snooping around them covertly?

Rit would keep on guard and investigate those looking into her. Lavender thought little of humans, though. The concealed figures were no different from annoying flies buzzing around. She would shoo them away, and if they proved particularly annoying, she'd swat them. Either way, her response always involved confrontation.

"I should warn you; I'm in a bit of a bad mood. Stomping a few ants might make me feel better." Lavender's tone was no bluff. Her words were entirely honest. It wasn't out of the question for her to attack at any moment.

Rit didn't falter, however. "Right, and without Van around, you can even get serious."

"What did you say?"

"I'm a Spirit Scout. I have the ability to control spirits... I can see that your little body is nothing more than a shadow of your true nature."

"Ohh..." Lavender's expression changed.

"Your true nature is a wild, gigantic power...the sort of presence that would terrify people."

"Say another word, and I'll kill you." The air around Lavender warped.

"Hey, hey. That aura reminds me of a dragon lord." Danan stepped forward to cover Rit, but she held out a hand to stop him.

"Which leads to the next question," Rit continued.

"What?"

Rit hoped for a proper conversation, not a one-sided speech.

She and Danan were dealing with a nonhuman who wouldn't hesitate to slaughter someone or break laws if she so desired.

Almost like the Hero..., Rit thought wryly.

"Why is a being so powerful, one who sees humans as so little, masking her true nature and pretending to be a little fairy?"

"..."

"If you didn't sense some worth in people, then what does it matter if they're terrified of you? Why do your utmost to hide your strength?"

Lavender seethed murderously, but she had yet to lash out. She glared at Rit, waiting for her to continue.

"It's because you love Van." Rit answered her own question in a clear voice. "Knowing that your true form is frightening to humans, you adopted one closer to the common human perception of a fairy so Van would love you."

There was a crackle.

"Here it comes!"

No sooner did Danan get the words out than an argent bolt struck in the alley, leaving scorch marks on the pavement and walls.

"Lightning Bolt? That's some pretty strong magic."

"She's a fay with an affinity for electricity, I guess."

Danan and Rit had dashed up the walls to avoid the lightning.

"You're the ones who attacked Van the other day."

"Oy, don't phrase it like he's the victim," Danan spat as he and Rit leaped down to the ground. "It turned into a fight because he tried to brainwash everyone in Zoltan."

"Everything Van does is right."

"Huh?"

Lavender didn't appear to be joking.

Her expression indicated she genuinely believed that.

Rit braced herself.

"Your name is Lavender, right?"

"Don't ask pointless questions when you've already gone snooping around."

Magic power gathered in the little fairy's body.

Danan readied himself for the next attack.

"Lavender! I want to talk with you!" Rit shouted.

"I don't have any interest in speaking to you. You can just die now."

Sensing a furious pressure from above, Danan prepared to grab Rit and run toward Lavender.

However...

"I'm in love, too. I want to talk about love with you!"

"Eh?"

Lavender stopped moving.

We're past the first hurdle...

For the first time, the fairy expressed some interest in Rit as an individual instead of viewing her as another faceless human.

Now Rit could finally begin a proper discussion.

Sensing the wind spirits that had gathered in the sky disperse, Rit exhaled in relief.

* * *

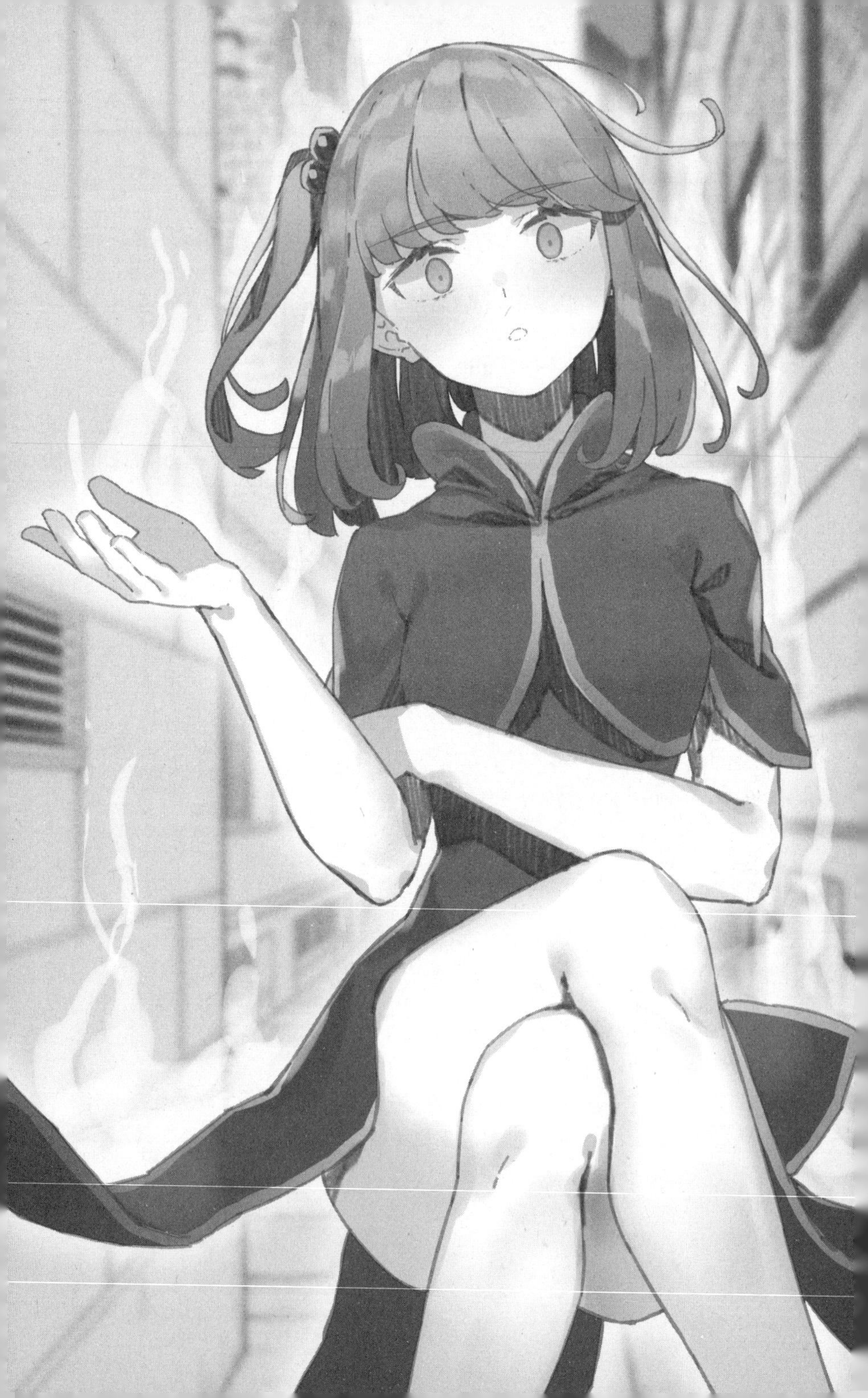

We're in uncharted territory now. I'll just have to think on my feet as we go.

Rit and Danan were on the first floor of the tavern where Van's party was staying.

"Is that man the one you love?"

Lavender pointed at Danan, but Rit smiled and shook her head.

"No, I run an apothecary here in town with the man I love."

"I'm just protection. I'll drink at the next table over, so you two can talk about whatever you want."

"I thought so. You look like someone who wouldn't understand love."

"Well, you got me pegged." Danan grinned as he took a seat. "Hey, miss, can I get a beer and some skewers?"

"Sure thing."

This was a comparatively cheap tavern. The food was the same sort found in the working-class part of Zoltan instead of the Central style more common downtown.

Rit was a little surprised that Van and his comrades would stay here, but set that aside to focus on Lavender.

"So, what is your name?"

"My name is Rit."

"Hmm, Rit, huh…?"

Lavender looked her up and down openly.

Her asking my name means she has at least a little interest in talking.

Rit watched Lavender's eyes while she considered how best to begin. *Hmm…*

After looking into Lavender's eyes momentarily, Rit decided to change course a bit.

That little fairy shape is a pretense; she's a being far older and more powerful than humans. Best not to lie, even by omission; she'll see through any tricks immediately…

Rit looked her straight in the eyes.

"Rit is just a nickname. My full name is Rizlet of Loggervia. I was a princess of the Duchy of Loggervia, which lies far to the north."

Danan's brow twitched slightly.

He didn't expect me to reveal myself. We're dealing with an enemy, after all. But I don't have a choice.

Fortunately, Danan's reaction was so minor that only one of his comrades would have noticed. His eyes remained fixed on the wooden mug of beer the waitress brought him.

Lavender leaned toward Rit.

"A princess, huh? I've read human stories about them. So is your lover a prince or a knight? Or is he a commoner you ran off with?"

"A knight from a foreign land… I gave up my royal life, and we live as commoners in this town."

"Right, if it's for love, then you don't need anything else!" Lavender said excitedly.

"You feel the same?" Rit asked.

Lavender nodded without hesitation. "Of course! I'd sacrifice anything and everything other than Van and myself!"

Both Rit and Lavender were in love, yet their thoughts on the matter were wholly different.

This was to be a battle of words in place of swords or magic. And just as a feint would not work against a vastly superior opponent, Rit couldn't fool Lavender with lies or misdirection.

"Hey, what is your lover like?"

Rit grinned. "He's kind, gallant, cool, and cute. His smile is wonderful. I love the way he blushes and gets a little awkward when I cling to him. And I also like how serious he gets during an important job, but I also enjoy his relaxed expressions when he takes it easy."

"All a bunch of likes. Then is there any part about him you hate?"

Lavender's eyes had a judging gleam—a dangerous sort of look that indicated negotiations might break down depending on how Rit answered.

Still, she didn't balk.

"No. I love everything about Red."

"But he must have faults."

"Yes, my Red has his faults. Yet I love everything about him. I want to be with him forever, even when we're old and gray. Until the very end. Is that the wrong answer?"

Lavender stared at Rit briefly before her small face broke into a satisfied smile. "No, you pass! I'll listen to your story!" Lavender raised her hand and shouted, "Mead and salad! Two each!" The little creature knocked her little hand on the table while demanding food.

She was a rude customer, but since she looked like a fairy, it probably came off as adorable to most.

The other tavern patrons burst into laughs.

Rit didn't find it amusing, however. Her heart was just as hot as when she held her swords in the thick of battle, but she did her best to remain coolheaded.

The victory condition is convincing her that leaving Zoltan without fighting Ruti is the best thing for Van.

Rit would have to battle Lavender's feelings with her own.

* * *

The fairy's affection was single-minded.

"Human love stories are wonderful, so why can't real humans live that way?"

Lavender's wings fluttered as she sat on the table. She drank from a small, handmade mug that she filled by scooping the mead out of a deep plate set in front of her.

Rit was drinking, too, slowly, so the alcohol didn't dull her judgment.

"If you've fallen in love, you shouldn't ever leave your beloved. You should've gone with him, regardless of his little sister."

"It's true. After they left Loggervia, I cried. And there were many nights I regretted not following after them."

"Exactly!"

Rit left out that Ruti was the Hero, but she did tell Lavender about how she and Red had fought together in Loggervia, their parting, and that they'd met again and opened a shop in Zoltan.

Lavender clearly enjoyed Rit's story, at times pressing her for more and always offering her own thoughts.

"Love is more blissful than anything! So if you fall in love, that feeling should be more important than anything else. Friends, your homeland, your family, anyone else's happiness—even that man's little sister. Your feelings are more important than all else. Destroy the world for them. That's true love."

Lavender had grown talkative, and as Rit conversed with her, she gradually got a sense of what the fairy desired from the Hero.

Just a little more, and I think I might understand completely...

"But you know, without me letting him go then, I don't think it would be possible for us to have the relationship we do now."

"Hmm?"

"Back then, Red and I lacked the capacity for something more. Had I gone with him, I don't think it would've been as fulfilling as the love we share today," Rit stated confidently.

She took careful note of Lavender's expression. Because they were both women in love, there were certainly some similarities. However, Rit also understood there was a fundamental difference in their perspectives.

Lavender appeared unsatisfied, but then her face brightened, as though she'd found the solution to a troubling problem.

"I get it. You weren't really in love yet in Loggervia!" Lavender spoke with as much certainty as Rit.

"You think? But I loved Red back in Loggervia, too."

"But you love the current Red, right?"

"I do."

"Then doesn't that mean you didn't love the old Red?"

"...How do you figure that?" Rit did her best to hide her rising irritation.

"Because the old Red and the current one are different. If you care about the present one, then it means you didn't feel anything for the old one."

"Couldn't you say that I loved the Red from back then, but here in Zoltan we both grew to love each other even more?"

"You can't. Love isn't something that develops. Love is a beautiful, blissful, perfect thing. The moment you are in love, you know it would be fine if time stopped and that moment continued forever. Love isn't true otherwise." Lavender made her argument without a trace of doubt in her voice.

"…"

Rit didn't accept that. This was the essential difference.

"Lavender, do you not want Van to change?"

"Of course not. I love him."

She loved him, so she wanted him to stay as he was. That was what Lavender desired from the Hero. So long as he obeyed the impulses of his blessing, he would remain the same.

I understand what Esta told us better now. Lavender constantly approves of everything Van does while rejecting Esta's suggestions, because she loves Van as he is presently. She doesn't want Van to grow, but that's just forcing her love on him.

Rit pitied Lavender.

She affirmed everything about Van and supported him always. She'd gladly throw away her life for him, in all likelihood. And even as she died, she would be happy to be of use to him.

It was a completely single-minded love, but it was one-way, and Lavender didn't truly love a real person. She cared for the ideal figure of Van she'd created. It was a love that was complete only within her mind.

"More mead!"

Lavender happily imbibed while listening to Rit's story.

"You know, I'm grateful for the love I've known. Because I'm completely happy."

"'Happy'?" Lavender stopped drinking to eye Rit. "Love is a happy thing, so it's only natural you are glad now."

"But when I was with Red in Loggervia, when I wasn't in love by your definition, I was happy then as well. From the bottom of my heart."

"You told me you worried and cried a lot, though."

"My love in Loggervia was painful and difficult, but now it's an irreplaceable memory…one of my dearest!"

"That doesn't make any sense."

Lavender shrugged indifferently. She didn't seem interested in understanding Rit's feelings.

Still, she didn't outright reject my views. I failed to land a finisher, but it could serve as a useful opener later.

Rit's final step was to explain her goal.

"You know, Lavender…"

"What?"

"Van is the Hero, so he's going to keep fighting lots of scary enemies."

"Yup! He's so cool!"

"But there are some really, really powerful creatures in the demon lord's army. Being the Hero isn't enough to guarantee he'll win."

"I know that."

Lavender didn't look particularly taken aback by Rit's statement. That wasn't surprising, but seeing the fairy so unmoved left Rit a little unsure about what to say next.

"…The Hero doesn't feel fear and can't abandon suffering people. So he can misjudge when best to flee from an unwinnable battle. Legends of previous bearers of the Hero blessing detail times when the Hero chose the wrong time to retreat and fell into danger or lost comrades."

"True, Van has shades of that quality."

"In one story, the Hero skirted peril because an ally advised they pull out…although that ally died fighting in the rear guard."

The tale was a myth, not documented history. None could speak to its veracity. Before Ruti, many people had believed the Hero blessing itself was a legend.

Regardless, it was clear that the story of the old Hero who had lost a comrade could easily repeat itself with Van. And just as Rit expected, Lavender nodded in agreement.

"Lavender, what would you do if Van insisted on staying to fight but there was no hope of victory? Could you save him even if it meant going against his wishes?"

Lavender stared into Rit's eyes for a few moments before grinning and shaking her head.

"I'd support Van."

"But he might die."

"I love Van. It's more important that he remains himself than anything else. And if he died for it…"

"What would you do?"

Lavender spread her arms and beamed. "I would die with him! I would love Van to my last breath. There's no happier story than that!"

"So that's how you feel."

This is all I can do for now.

"Lavender, I have a request for you."

"A request? Nope, nope. I don't take orders from humans other than Van."

"I understand, but this is for him."

"Hmmm. Really? It was a tiny bit interesting talking with you. Go ahead and ask, then."

Lavender put her mug down on the table and focused on Rit. Her smile was gone.

Danan, still at the next table over, got ready to fight at a moment's notice.

Rit kept a calm demeanor as she spoke. "I want you to tell Van that he should leave Zoltan."

"…"

"The girl that Van wants to fight is very strong. Van might lose and die."

Lavender didn't get angry. Whether Van the Hero was the strongest didn't matter to her. The fairy kept silent and listened.

"This isn't a battle worth risking his life for. If he wins, his blessing level will increase a bit, that's all. The result would be no different than if he fought some monster or members of the demon lord's army."

"That is certainly true." Lavender nodded. "But I refuse, of course."

"I thought you'd say that."

"Hah-hah! Good! I thought I might have to kill you to get you to back off!"

Lavender understood that Rit's reasoning was correct from a logical cost-benefit standpoint. However, Lavender's goal was to love Van as he was in the moment. She'd never try to change his mind to spare him from danger.

That's enough for now. She's not someone I can convince in a single meeting. It's enough that I conveyed my intent even though we're at odds.

A giant monster that couldn't be slain in one battle might still go down after multiple fights.

"Then before we leave…" Rit raised her mug.

"Oh, I know this! It's a strange human custom! But aren't you supposed to do it before drinking?" Lavender raised her little cup anyway.

"Here's hoping that we'll be able to chat in peace again sometime. Cheers."

"This not-quite-a-promise, not-really-a-prayer thing is weird, but cheers."

The two of them finished their drinks in one go and stood.

* * *

The riding drake racetrack at the north of town saw a lot of gambling. The drakes running weren't racing thoroughbreds. They belonged to knights and were usually ridden into combat or used as beasts of burden. They weren't trained for this sort of competition.

Thus, it wasn't rare for a drake to pitch a fit and stop running before reaching the finish line. Races held on weekends were mostly for raising prize money distributed to offset the high costs of maintaining riding drakes. So even though people gambled on them, most spectators just watched without getting too attached to any single outcome.

If someone saw the drake they'd bet on stop partway down the track and buck the jockey frantically trying to get their mount moving again, they'd laugh. There was no point in getting upset and wasting one's ticket.

One outsider in attendance was not so easygoing, though…

"Damn it all! This is rigged! Give me my money back!"

Ljubo clenched his ticket as he shouted.

I couldn't help but think he'd be an annoying customer if he ever visited my shop, but I was also a little relieved. Ljubo was a worldly sort, making him far easier to work with than a zealot.

"So how do you want to approach this, Red?" Yarandrala asked from beside me.

Our goal was to convince Ljubo.

He was in the middle of a hideous display unbefitting a cleric, but he knew he could cut loose a bit this far from Central. Simply put, this was his genuine personality.

"His judgment will be worse when he's annoyed. Let's go now."

"Got it."

Yarandrala and I approached Ljubo in disguise.

He shouldn't be able to see through nonmagical alterations.

"Your Eminence."

Ljubo spun around upon hearing my voice. He glared at me with eyes a little bloodshot from the excitement.

"What do you want? I'm off today! If you need me, then save it for tomorrow!"

I hadn't known the Hero's party was entitled to days off, but I resisted the urge to comment on that.

Maybe I'm the weird one for assuming there was no room for leisure... I probably shouldn't dwell on that too much.

"The truth is, we have a little tidbit for you, Your Eminence."

I spoke with the voice of Waverly, a thief whose identity I'd assumed before. The voice should be foreign to Ljubo, and the real Waverly was in prison.

"What? I'm not interested!"

Still caught up in his indignation, Ljubo turned away to watch the drakes lined up for the next race.

This man hardly wanted for money, but he probably enjoyed increasing his fortune anyway. Such a desire better suited a lord or merchant than a holy man.

"Don't be like that."

"Leave me be!"

Thud!

Ljubo shoved me away, and I fell to the ground without resisting.

"Hmph!"

After sparing me a brief look, Ljubo smirked and departed.

"Red, are you okay?"

"Of course."

There was no way that would hurt me.

After standing, I waited a bit before pursuing Ljubo.

"Feh, they all look awful!" Ljubo grumbled as he observed the riding drakes assembled in the waiting area.

Discerning whether a normal riding drake was suited to racing required a different sense and knowledge than determining which of a group of race-trained drakes were better or worse.

"Your Eminence, I would recommend number five."

I approached Ljubo while pointing to a drake that had just let out a big yawn.

"You again?"

Ljubo glared at me, but then he looked at the drake I pointed to.

"It looks a little fat to my eyes."

"You shouldn't judge by racing drake standards. That one's a serious drake, and it has stamina. For this track, where the drakes don't know their jockeys or the pacing for a race, those are the best traits to have."

"Hrmm…"

Hearing that, Ljubo looked closer at the drake.

"Are you not going to bet on it?"

"Of course. I've already placed my bet." I pulled a ticket from my pocket.

"Hmph… Well, fine, then."

Ljubo headed over to buy a ticket.

Seeing that, Yarandrala whispered in my ear.

"Red, is this all right? If this doesn't work out, we'll miss our opening."

"I was a vice-captain of the Bahamut Knights, remember? I have an eye for riding drakes. Just wait and see," I responded confidently.

I wasn't lying. That drake was my pick for this race.

But I was the only one who knew that Mister Crawly Wawly was standing on its head, brimming with confidence.

That riding drake was his friend.

✻   ✻   ✻

"Hah-hah, that was a good win." Ljubo was in a great mood. He didn't seem to be on guard at all as he followed after us. "The sweet drink of victory is best savored with flair. If you bring me to a dirty little hole in the wall, I'll have your nails ripped off," he added with a laugh. I got the feeling it wasn't a joke, however.

For now, I maintained my ingratiating smile.

"We've arrived, Your Eminence."

After a little walk, we reached the mansion where Rit used to live.

"Hmm? This looks almost like a noble's manor. Is there really a bar in a place like this?"

"Yes, we have an exquisite collection of liquors prepared."

"Ohhh."

I'd expected to put in more work to convince Ljubo, but he entered without hesitation.

"That's quite the confidence..."

It spoke to his belief that he could deal with anything that might happen. Ljubo didn't carry a weapon, but I knew he had an item box in his pocket. No member of the Hero's party was weak.

After bracing myself, I followed Ljubo inside.

* * *

"What, are you pouring?"

Yarandrala had changed into a trim bartender outfit and stood behind the counter set up in the building.

"She's a pro when it comes to drinks," I responded, sitting down next to Ljubo.

Yarandrala flashed a gleaming smile and bowed.

She'd once led an armed merchant fleet, after all. Sure, her goal was hunting pirates, but the merchant fleet's primary business had been hauling and selling cargo. Yarandrala had picked up a lot about alcohol during that part of her life.

"Hmph, well, give me your best drink to start with." Ljubo scowled.

The manor was stocked with many high-class wines, brandies, whiskeys, and other popular liquors that could be found in Zoltan. But those were only there in case Ljubo requested a specific drink. Our first choice was something quite different.

"Then how about this wine?"

"Hmm? Serving a wine that hasn't been bottled..."

Ljubo's face twisted further upon his seeing that Yarandrala was pouring red liquid from a leather pouch.

Wine quickly oxidized, and its flavor deteriorated when exposed to the air. It was normal to bottle wine fresh out of the cask and seal it with a cork.

"The aroma is quite good, but a wine kept so crudely couldn't possibly appease my palate."

Presumably, the only thing keeping Ljubo from standing was the first-rate aroma coming from the glass. Ljubo raised his cup to observe the drink's color.

"The shade is good. I see. The appearance certainly rivals that of a high-grade wine."

And then Ljubo emptied the glass in a single gulp.

"Mrgh, hrmm…" Suddenly, he went stiff.

Yarandrala smiled, knowing it had worked.

"To think there was such a delicious wine in this backwater!"

Ljubo made no effort to hide his shock as he sniffed the remnant fragrance from the glass.

"The attack is so simple, yet there is a subtle complexity to it. There's an unmistakably strong fruity mellowness to it, but, hmmm… I detect a sophisticated balance between the richness and tartness. It leans sweeter, but the aftertaste is clean and refreshing. And the alcohol asserts itself without being overpowering. The texture is like a luxurious silk, and more than anything the intensity of the aftertaste reminds me of an elegant lady-in-waiting who casts off her dress and dances unrestrained in the forest! This is a truly wonderful wine!"

Ljubo was off on a rant.

I'd heard he loved to drink expensive alcohol. Acquiring some fairy wine had proven the right choice.

This was what I had gone to Undine for the other day. I figured someone who had spent his entire life with the church would never have tasted something prepared by the fay before. Fortunately, the plan worked, and Ljubo was surprised.

"Then please, have a second glass and enjoy it with this fish-based dish." Yarandrala placed some *oden* in front of Ljubo. Oparara had made it for us this morning.

"This is fish?"

Ljubo cocked his head while eyeing the cake made of pounded fish and *chikuwa*.

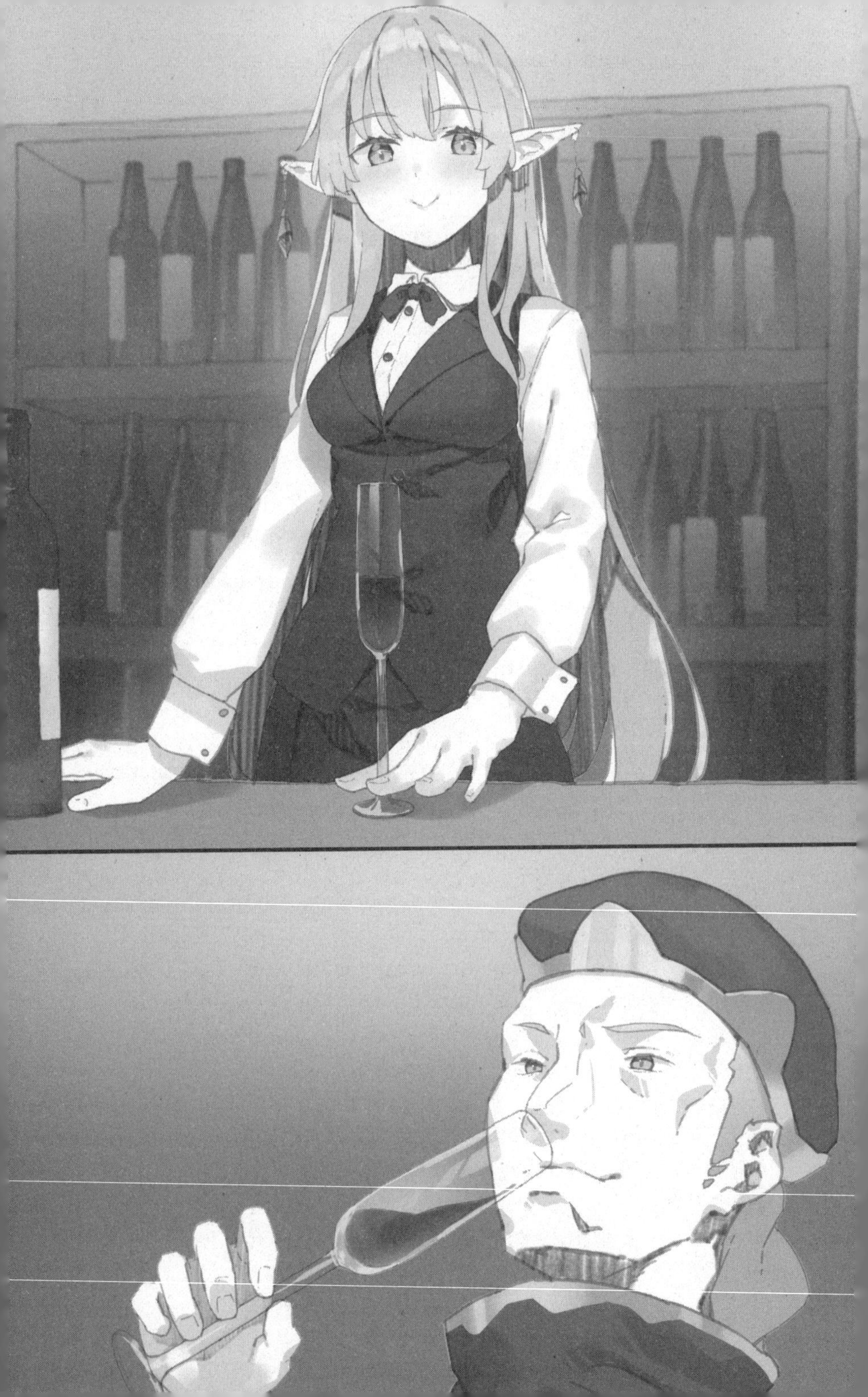

"It is made from grated fish."

"Hmmm."

Ljubo had a dubious look on his face as he bit into the *chikuwa*. "Mrgh!" His eyes widened.

"It pairs excellently with wine as well."

At Yarandrala's suggestion, Ljubo took a sip of the wine after swallowing the *chikuwa*.

"Hah-hah. This is why I always find myself traveling away from the church. You'd never find such magnificent wine and food at the Last Wall fortress." Ljubo nodded to himself in satisfaction while taking another bite. "This rich soup and the red wine are quite the serendipitous pair. It's common for alcohol and dishes from the same land to go well together, but to think a food this different would partner so excellently with this wine. I must admit…this is a combination even I find satisfying."

The cardinal enjoyed his meal in good spirits.

The fairy wine and foreign dish had moved him, and that was enough to rob him of his presence of mind. Naturally, the alcohol helped, too.

We can't let him get so drunk that he forgets where he is, though. It's best to get him right at that spot where he's suggestible but lucid.

I watched Ljubo carefully while Yarandrala and I offered him more wine until he'd had just enough.

I think that should do it…

Approaching the cardinal in disguise, leading him to Rit's old mansion, and plying him with food and drink were all to ensure I began the negotiation from as advantageous a position as possible.

Such was the tactic of one with no special skills or magic. Put another way, I had to resort to this, or I'd never succeed.

Something similar had happened a while back, when I'd slacked off on my research and messed up an application to sell anesthetic in Zoltan. I only got approval thanks to Rit's connections, and I wanted to believe I'd learned from that error.

"Are you satisfied with our offering, Your Eminence?"

"It was pretty good. So, then, shall I head out?"

"You should rest a little longer, at least until you are no longer impaired from the drink," I said while passing Ljubo a glass of water.

"Hmph, letting the buzz fade would be a waste."

He wanted more wine, not water.

He had finished the last of the fairy wine, so next was a premium wine that could be bought in Zoltan.

"Ahhh, this is heaven."

He swirled the glass of red wine as he said that.

That's not something a man of the cloth should be saying.

"What's with that look? Do you doubt a cardinal of the holy church's words? The Lord Demis created wine, so what problem is there in finding the divine in alcohol?"

It was an absurd statement, but the ease and confidence with which he said it was almost enough to make me believe him.

I guess this is the charisma of a man who's fought his way to the top of the continent's biggest organization.

"There is a small thing I'd like to discuss with Your Eminence, if I might. Naturally, you are free to continue enjoying your wine in the meantime."

"Good, good. I'll allow it. As thanks for the good drink and food," he answered arrogantly.

"It concerns Van the Hero, whom you watch over."

Ljubo took that in stride without batting an eye, as though he'd expected this topic to come up. "He is the Hero who will someday save the world. I'm afraid I must ask you to suffer some inconvenience for him." Ljubo waved his hand lightly.

He'd anticipated a request to do something about Van. This was likely not his first time hearing a grievance about the boy.

Everyone in Zoltan found Van unpleasant, so it wasn't surprising that people had come to Ljubo with complaints. Undoubtedly, it was too frightening to talk with Van directly, so his guardian was the next-best option.

Zoltan's peace meant nothing to Ljubo, though. Whatever happened out here wouldn't alter his standing. The cardinal valued his relationship with Van and Van's reputation more. From his perspective, the trouble the Hero had caused in Zoltan wasn't anything to fret over.

"While I will compliment you on the warm reception, I cannot do anything," Ljubo said as he started to stand.

"Please wait a moment, Your Eminence. We actually wish to convey the danger of the opponent the Hero intends to confront."

Ljubo stiffened at my remark. "What did you say?"

He typically would've dismissed such a statement as specious, especially when it came from a stranger. However, the fairy wine had moved him. Even someone as self-centered as Ljubo wished to do something for the person who had granted him such an affecting experience.

The man wasn't so foolish as to believe every word without question, but he was willing to listen for a moment.

"Very well. I can't promise anything, but I'll at least hear you out." He sat back down, and I poured him a new glass of wine.

"It is about the being that defeated Van the Hero."

"Hmmm, you speak as though you know something. Who was this enemy?"

I'd been working out an answer to that question for the past week.

Linking the event to Ruti was dangerous. Hardly anyone saw her using her full strength, but her power was well-known enough that she was the first person people thought of when asked who Zoltan's strongest adventurer was. Ljubo wouldn't accept that a B-rank adventurer in the middle of nowhere was so mighty as to best the Hero, though.

I had to cite something more plausible.

"It was a remnant of the ancient elves."

"Huh?" Ljubo looked dubious. "Don't be stupid. The ancient elves only left behind those mechanical clockwork creatures. It was a human girl who defeated Van."

"Naturally, my word is insufficient for one so discerning. Please, this way." After standing, I glanced at Ljubo's glass of wine.

"Hmph..."

He drained the glass in one go and followed me to the basement. His gait was just a little bit wobbly.

※　　　　　※　　　　　※

"It has been some time since it died…so please forgive the stench."

"'Died'? Is there a corpse down here?"

I opened the door to a small room in the basement.

"That's not something to smell after eating." Ljubo's face puckered up as a terrible stench wafted out the door.

"It was preserved to prevent decay."

I opened the lid of a plain casket lying on the floor.

"…An ogrekin? Hmm, but its body is shaped differently."

"It is a mutant ogrekin."

Within the coffin was one of the ogrekin that Rit and I had fought in Sant Durant.

"Please, observe the markings on its neck, Your Eminence." I pointed to the characters printed on the dead creature's nape.

"Ancient elf script? Did you write that?"

"Not at all. This was written while the monster was alive—before it matured, even."

"I see…"

"Tattooing a ferocious ogrekin while alive would be difficult. And close inspection should reveal this is no ordinary mark. Some unknown technique was used to embed the color in the deepest levels of the skin."

"'Unknown technique'… Then you believe this is the result of genuine ancient elf work?"

"I do. There is an ancient elf ruin in the mountains to the northwest of Zoltan. My theory is that this monster originated there."

The most convincing lie was one that ran close to the truth. Changing the fewest details possible decreased possible conflicts with reality. A lie would never be uncovered if it didn't clash with the facts.

"That's... No, the proof is here before my eyes."

Ljubo had forgotten the stench, and he leaned in to examine the corpse.

Ogrekin were known to have a link to the ancient elves.

The more the cardinal inspected, the more concrete my story became.

"This is indeed ancient elven writing. And this monster bears different characteristics from an ordinary ogrekin."

Ljubo undoubtedly harbored suspicions about Van's defeat. Why would a being capable of beating the Hero to within an inch of his life reside in the middle of nowhere? Such a being surely would have used their power to become wealthy and famous.

By the very nature of Divine Blessings, a mighty blessing had to possess an important role.

Any blessing capable of defeating the Hero ought to be making waves in Central.

Hopefully, an ancient elven reason would make a hardened, experienced cardinal believe otherwise.

"But a human attacked Van..."

"Yes, this ogrekin is just one species the ancient elves altered. While it would make for a powerful opponent for Zoltan adventurers, it's no match for the Hero."

"So there's another kind?"

"Yes, Your Eminence. And that's what defeated the Hero. Have you heard a report on Queen Leonor's war with Zoltan?"

"The gist, but I've not been informed of the details."

Information on events in Zoltan usually didn't make it to Central. Even the most detailed accounts likely only covered events up to Bishop Shien's departure, before the fighting broke out.

"This is a report regarding everything that occurred in Zoltan." I handed Ljubo a stack of papers.

"Thieves Guild documents?"

Ljubo read through the file.

Although the report appeared to be from the Thieves Guild, I'd drafted it specifically to show to the cardinal. There were no lies, but I'd excluded some inconvenient facts while emphasizing some trivial points to misdirect Ljubo.

"Cutting a giant galleon in half?"

"It should still be sitting beneath the water, if you wish to see it."

"…No, no need."

He believes me. That's a good sign.

"I thought the victory was thanks to Veronian Admiral Lilinrala's efforts."

"That wasn't a battle a single galley could win, even when helmed by the legendary captain of the Elven Corsairs. It was the strength of a mysterious humanoid that won the day."

"Remarkable."

I'd written of Ruti's efforts during the fight while minimizing what Rit, Tisse, and I had done to make her feats stand out all the more.

Upon seeing Ljubo's tense expression, I knew I'd successfully planted the idea of a dangerous being that could defeat the Hero.

"Why did this monster intervene in the naval skirmish with Veronia?"

"I cannot begin to comprehend how a surviving piece of ancient elf handiwork thinks, but…I could speculate."

"Tell me."

"As best we can discern, this creature has taken action three times."

"Three?"

"Yes, Your Eminence. Once against Van the Hero, and another time during the fight with Veronia."

"And the third?"

"Fifty years ago, when the remnants of Goblin King Mulgarga's forces attacked Zoltan."

That part was a lie shuffled into the mix.

Ljubo had no way of knowing what had befallen Zoltan half a century ago, and it would be difficult to investigate the claim. All that was known was that Zoltan had managed to drive back Mulgarga's band. Of course, Mistorm and her crew were the ones who had actually saved Zoltan back then, but there was no need to tell Ljubo that.

"Zoltan is a peaceful land. Until recently, there was no major trouble here after the goblins were driven off."

"So this surviving piece of ancient elf handiwork safeguards Zoltan in times of peril?"

"Close, but I believe the truth is slightly different. Take note that it didn't act during the Devil's Blessing trouble from a few months back."

In the aftermath of that incident, Ruti had encountered a contract demon, which brought her to Zoltan. Obviously, she couldn't have been involved because she hadn't been here before that, but that was all kept secret from Ljubo.

"I've concentrated my efforts on determining how that Devil's Blessing crisis differed from the other three."

"I don't know anything about a backwater so disconnected from the rest of the continent, so don't bother with the windup, and tell me your conclusion."

"Essentially, the Devil's Blessing incident threatened the state of Zoltan because of a potential coup d'état, but the others were massive martial dangers. The ancient elf creation was likely drawn out by the salt dragon attack and judged Van the Hero a powerful threat to be dealt with."

"I see. Of course. Zoltan didn't exist during the time of the ancient elves, so perhaps the creature was a guardian to protect this region."

Ljubo nodded in acceptance.

Great.

"It is quite the powerful warrior in the face of an impending attack on Zoltan. Were forces from the demon lord's army to land here, the ancient elf creation would surely rise to meet the monsters in battle."

"That seems likely… So do you mean to suggest Van ought to withdraw for the sake of humanity?"

"Indeed. Your Eminence is rearing Van the Hero to be strong

enough to fight the demon lord's army. However, something so valuable as a piece of ancient elf handiwork shouldn't be risked for such preparations. Were the Hero to die fighting it, that would of course be a terrible loss to humanity. And it would also be a tragic loss for the ancient marvel to perish."

Ljubo kept Van from engaging the demon lord's forces to ensure the boy was strong enough to survive the fight. Hopefully, he'd understand that my argument followed similar thinking.

The problem was whether he would believe me. I'd done all I could to that end. The rest was up to Ljubo.

"What is your name?"

"Me, Your Eminence? My name is Waverly."

Waverly was the name of one of Bighawk's henchmen. I'd disguised myself as him in the past.

Rather than create a new persona, it was safer to model an identity after an existing person. There was less chance of an obvious contradiction.

"Your logic is sound… I will advise Van that we should leave Zoltan right away."

Yes!

Satisfied, Yarandrala and I exchanged a glance. Ljubo looked strange, though.

"Is there a problem, Your Eminence?"

"I will advise it… I will, but…" Ljubo wore a troubled look and shook his head. "Lately, Van does not listen to me…"

"Is Van not the church's Hero?"

"He is. At least, he was supposed to be. However, Van is closer to Almighty Demis than an average person."

"But you are the only one who can lead Van where he needs to go, Your Eminence."

"Indeed… I shall attempt to speak with him. If you learn anything more about this ancient elf creation, let me know. You know where I am staying in town, correct?"

"Yes, Your Eminence. If we discover anything, you will be the first to hear of it."

"Mmh. I'm counting on you," Ljubo replied, as though issuing an order to a servant.

This went about as well as we could've hoped.

Chapter 3
And Sometimes I'm Not Sure

The next day, Rit, Ruti, Tisse, Yarandrala, Danan, Esta, Albert, and I gathered in Yarandrala's room at the inn where she was staying.

"That's the rundown of things from the past few days."

Everyone nodded after Rit and I delivered our reports.

"'An ancient elven creation,' huh?" Esta chuckled a bit.

She was much more expressive than before she'd donned her mask.

"You really come up with some unexpected ideas. And seeing an utterly convinced Ljubo trying to sell Van on it was excellent."

"I'm just amazed that you were able to deceive Cardinal Ljubo, of all people, with a story like that," Albert said with admiration.

"Ljubo and I both argued that we should leave Zoltan, but Lavender and Van are set on staying and searching for Ruti. Although in Lavender's case, she's simply supporting Van's decision and probably doesn't see any point in fighting Ruti," Esta explained.

"So far, everything's going as expected," I replied.

Swaying Ljubo had denied Van help in his hunt for Ruti. And without such an influential church member aiding him, Van had no option but to search for Ruti directly on his own. The current plan was to use the extra time that afforded us so Rit could win over Lavender.

"The talk with Lavender could've gone worse, but her single-minded love makes her a challenge," Rit said.

"Ljubo won't be an issue so long as we maintain contact, so we should focus on Van and Lavender."

"There's at least some hope for convincing Lavender, but what about Van?"

Esta shook her head. "His behavior has grown odd since the encounter with Ruti. Before, he would listen when Ljubo insisted, but now…"

"So the Hero is hung up on killing Ruti?" Danan groaned.

Hmm…

"I understand his belief that the Hero blessing's urges are just and that to satisfy one's blessing is a sign of devotion to God's teachings, and thus, the right course of action. But is he really so devoted to beating Ruti just because he wants to increase his level?" I asked.

To raise one's blessing level was to act in accordance with God, who assigned that blessing. Valuing that endeavor highly was in line with Van's sense of virtue. However, if the goal was simply to increase his blessing, there was no need to seek out Ruti specifically. Van could fight any powerful enemy with a blessing, as he'd done in the south seas.

"Hard to say. It's not like I know anyone else's blessing." Danan didn't seem interested in thinking about it, either, as his fist thudded against his knee. "Not bein' able to fight wears on my nerves!"

"You're our trump card if a battle becomes inevitable, so you'll have to put up with it for now," I said.

We couldn't let Ruti fight, so Danan was our strongest usable combatant. He was the only one who could stop Van alone.

Danan cocked an eyebrow. "Really? Couldn't you figure something out for a guy like him?"

"Don't be crazy. He held his ground fighting you and Yarandrala simultaneously," I responded.

"If it weren't for those salt dragons, we woulda murdered him then and there," Danan grumbled.

It would be really problematic if you actually killed him, so could you not focus on that?

"…Anyway, the Hero is the hope of the people. Even if Van doesn't really live up to that ideal," Esta said. "I don't intend to force him to try to save the world just because he's the Hero, but if his power causes trouble for others, then it's our duty as party members to the last Hero to guide him, right?"

I nodded. "Right... For now, let's take things one step at a time. First is convincing Lavender. Rit, continue leading efforts on that front, and the rest of us will do whatever we can to support her."

"Yeah, I'll be counting on you all," Rit answered with a smile.

Ruti pouted as she watched us. "There's nothing for me to do."

We had to keep Van from finding her, so she was being kept in reserve as an absolute last resort—to be used only if someone's life was in genuine danger. Naturally, we were doing our best to keep things from reaching that point, so ideally, Ruti would never take action at all.

"Everyone else is doing so much." We smiled as Ruti grumbled in frustration.

"Your job is to protect our day-to-day lives. We're entrusting you with watching the shop and the plantation while Tisse, Rit, and I aren't around."

"Ah, that is important." Ruti's eyes widened, and she broke into a smile. "Leave the store to me. I've memorized where all the medicines go and their effects."

"Good. I'm counting on you."

"Mhm."

Customers had been inconvenienced while we were away on our vacation, so I didn't want to close the shop again if I could help it. If Ruti was willing to pitch in, I'd gladly accept her help.

"Wait." Yarandrala spoke up for the first time during the meeting. Her tone was sharp. "Van is on the move!"

She'd been monitoring the Hero's activities via her ability to communicate with plants.

Once Yarandrala got to know the vegetation of an area, the range of her network exceeded that of skills or standard forms of magical detection.

"And they're heading this way!" Yarandrala added.

"Lavender's caught on to us."

It was likely the same technique that had allowed the fairy to notice Tisse while she was hidden. We'd have to hold our next meeting at Red & Rit's Apothecary.

I quickly handed out instructions with a serious look on my face.

*   *   *

A bell chimed as the door to the shop opened.

There were two sets of footsteps, but three presences.

"Welcome," Rit greeted from behind the counter.

"Rit," Lavender replied.

"Hello, Lavender. And Van and Cardinal Ljubo as well."

"That big guy from last time, Esta, Albert, and Tisse are here, too, aren't they?"

"..."

"Playing dumb?"

"No, I'm a little surprised, but yes, they're all here, just like you said."

"See? I told you!" Lavender puffed out her little chest in boast. "Esta is connected with Rit! She betrayed us!"

"Mrgh." Ljubo sounded uncomfortable.

"Betrayed? She hasn't led you into a trap. Do you really think Esta would do that?" Rit said.

Lavender crossed her arms. "She's sneaking around behind our backs, isn't she?!"

"This isn't something to discuss in the middle of the store... Esta's inside, so why don't we all talk about it together?" Rit kept her cool as she spoke. Lavender didn't seem pleased by that reaction, but Ljubo looked relieved.

As for Van...

"Huh, there sure are a lot of medicines... Oh, let's get some of this one before we go."

Chapter 3: And Sometimes I'm Not Sure

Van innocently perused the items lined up on the shelves.

Rit led the three guests into the living room, where Esta, Albert, and Tisse waited.

"Where's the big guy?" Lavender questioned.

"Heh... This room's a bit small for both him and Cardinal Ljubo, so he's waiting somewhere else," Esta replied. Then she looked at Van. "I'm prepared to explain myself, but I gather you don't believe I've betrayed you."

Van cocked his head. "Not exactly. You're going to justify yourself, right? I can wait until I know if you've turned on us before treating you as an enemy."

The lack of concern in his voice was evident. His personality had become less human than before.

"Esta! Confess that you betrayed us and admit that Van should kill you on the spot!" Lavender insisted.

"No violence in the shop, please."

"Quiet! Van is always right, so he can cut someone down whenever he likes! No one can get in his way!"

Rit smiled wryly. "What a troublesome fairy."

"It won't come to that," Esta responded. "It's hurtful to be accused of betrayal. Cardinal Ljubo asked me to look into the identity of Van's enemy. It's only natural I'd reach out to someone well versed in the subject."

"'Well versed'?"

"Ljubo should have been given the report, too. The thieves he met work for Rit."

"What?"

Rit's expression was one of supreme confidence as she spoke to Ljubo. "I used to work as an adventurer. They were agents of a Thieves Guild faction I crushed."

That was a lie we'd cooked up, and Rit spoke it without hesitation.

"I got in touch with Esta, as my subordinates did with you, Your Eminence. And I convinced her there was no need for Van to fight the ancient elf creation."

"Mgh."

"Esta acted for Van's sake, and you, of all people, ought to see the reason not to battle that creature, Cardinal Ljubo."

"Yes, well…" Ljubo looked troubled. Lavender gnashed her teeth but kept silent.

All right. Ruti and Yarandrala should be far enough away by now. At the very least, they were beyond my detection. *Guess that means it's about time.*

*   *   *

"You sure this is all right, Red?" Danan whispered.

We were hiding together in the workroom, listening to the discussion with Van's party.

"I planned to observe how Rit's talk with Lavender proceeded, but this is a good chance for us to act."

Danan grinned. "It'll be a definite shock either way. Landing an opening punch after a feint is always a sweet feeling."

Martial arts remained his go-to for metaphors, even in tense situations.

"Okay, shall we?"

"Yeah."

Danan and I exited the workroom silently.

I could hear Rit skillfully parrying Lavender's high-pitched complaints in the living room.

"Is someone there?" Van asked, his voice directed at the door to where Danan and I were.

"It's that big guy. Guess he's coming out after all!" Lavender stomped noisily on the table.

"I wonder if you know him, Cardinal Ljubo…?" There was a slight trace of concern in Rit's voice.

She said *him*, not *them*, despite knowing Danan and I were hiding together. It was a covert question, asking if it was truly all right for me to go through with this. Honestly, it probably wasn't, but we were dealing with the Hero. I had to steel myself and take a risk.

"…Got it," Rit murmured softly, and then she turned to Van with a sharpness to her gaze. "Allow me to introduce the man I told Lavender about, the man I love. Red, could you come in, please?"

I opened the door.

"You're the swordsman who stole my shield!"

Van reached for his sword. But a loud voice thundered through the room as though to stop the Hero.

"It can't be! Why are Gideon and Danan here?!"

Lavender and Van froze upon seeing Ljubo's shock.

"Gideon and Danan… You mean…the warriors from Ruti the Hero's party?!"

"Indeed! These two fought alongside Ruti the Hero at the Last Wall fortress!"

Van had not shown any interest in the discussion thus far, but now we had his complete attention.

Hopefully, that would help him and his allies forget any possible connection between Esta, Tisse, and Rit beyond what had been explained already. Van believed in the Divine Blessing of the Hero above all else. Thus, Danan and I, the other Hero's comrades, were possibly the only two capable of influencing Van.

"Why—why are Ruti the Hero's comrades here?!"

Danan and I glanced at each other.

"See for yourself."

Danan held up his right arm and rolled back his sleeve, revealing his missing forearm.

"I screwed up."

"That's…" Ljubo was speechless. He'd witnessed Danan's strength for himself during the battle at the Last Wall fortress.

"They're the ones who fought Van before the ancient elf creation arrived," Esta stated.

Tisse nodded. "Ruti the Hero's comrades would be able to fight Van on equal footing…"

"I reached out to them for information. There's no harm in paying respect to those who have fought the demon lord's army."

"And as a local adventurer, I knew they were staying in Zoltan, so of course I came to them for help occasionally."

Esta and Tisse both fibbed expertly, and Van accepted it at face value.

"I see. So that's how it happened."

Okay. That takes care of any suspicion regarding Esta and Tisse meeting with us. Let's deal with each problem in turn.

"So why did Ruti the Hero's comrades attack me?" Van looked genuinely confused.

A vein throbbed on Danan's temple.

Not good!

Before he exploded, I stepped in to explain. "It's because you were going to harm many people."

"'Harm'?"

"The Hero fights to save the suffering. We have left the Hero's party, but we still wish to protect the people of Zoltan from undue pain."

"You misunderstand. I acted because I wanted to rescue everyone from their doubt and allow them to live in accordance with their blessings and the teachings of Demis."

"That may be your way, but it wasn't how Ruti did things."

"Ruti the Hero…"

"Being manipulated by magic, seeing those dear to you die, losing your homeland, the Hero should prevent such tragedies, not cause them," I argued.

Van watched me, apparently unable to accept my words.

"I'm the Hero. My blessing's impulses tell me that what I'm doing is correct."

"And I'm the Guide. The one and only person in this world tasked with showing the Hero the proper way."

"That's…"

For the first time, Van was at a loss for how to respond. For just a moment, doubt ran across his eyes. My existence, my Guide blessing, was the ultimate challenge to Van's ideology of dogmatic adherence to blessings and religion. The Guide blessing was the one and only blessing created expressly for directing the Hero.

That was the biggest reason I'd elected to reveal my identity to Van. I was possibly the only person left who might convince the boy.

"Van, I think I need to have a talk with you."

"..."

Van looked unsure. His Divine Blessing was the pillar that supported his every decision, but he couldn't reject what I said because my blessing was meant to advise his.

A small figure abruptly stood between us.

"Don't trick Van! Van is always right!"

"Lavender."

"No, Rit! I won't let anyone get in the way of my love!"

Rit and Lavender stared each other down. Yet while the fairy glared hard at us, the malice in her eyes weakened when she looked at Rit. At least, that's how it appeared to me.

"I have no intention of getting in the way of your love... I only want to introduce you."

"..."

Rit broke into a tranquil smile. "This is the man I love."

"...I see."

"Lavender."

"What?"

"The simple life I share with Red is my love. And I won't let anyone threaten it."

"...!!!" Lavender was visibly stunned. The fairy had a very extreme outlook that differed from Van's.

No philosophical argument would alter Lavender's opinion. The only way to get through to her was by using the same perspective of love.

"We got to know each other a bit the other day. And today has been a meaningful encounter for all of us. Why don't we end things here for now?" I proposed.

"..."

Lavender kept her narrowed eyes trained on Rit, but she moved to Van's shoulder.

"Oh-ho." Ljubo was evidently surprised to see Lavender back down. "I suppose I should've expected nothing less of a Hero's comrades. I take it you will arrange a later meeting?"

I nodded. "Yes, it'd be best to speak with both sides on an even footing, don't you think?"

"I do indeed… Any objections, Van?"

"No…" Van was listless, still lost in contemplation.

*   *   *

Van's party left peacefully, and the living room in Red & Rit's Apothecary was silent for a bit.

"Should we really have let them go?" Tisse asked. "With more pressure, you might have been able to convince Van while he was still confused."

I shook my head.

"I might have been able to win him over momentarily, but it wouldn't have lasted."

The pillar of his faith was still unshakable.

We needed proper discourse, not deception. Van wouldn't give up on Ruti until he had an answer that suited his faith-based perspective.

"Is there any solution that will actually satisfy him?" Tisse inquired.

"That's a good question…," I said.

I figured Van would probably listen to me once I brought up my blessing, but there had never been a chance to broach the subject before because he had never been willing to spare a moment to listen.

"It sure looked like you were seeing a dozen moves ahead of them and leading them around by the nose…"

I smiled. "Making it look that way is just a negotiation tactic."

Truthfully, I had not been nearly so at ease as I'd made it seem in the moment. Lavender's ability to sense people limited coordination, which caused a lot of problems. I'd tried assembling our group in the apothecary shop, which was far from downtown, yet even that was apparently in range. Even if we concealed my and Danan's identities, it would be challenging for all of us to gather and exchange information in the future. Thus, I had to reveal our identities to remove Lavender's suspicion over our meeting.

"We obviously couldn't reveal that Lavender was giving us trouble. It was far better to make it seem like everything was proceeding as we planned. Still…that was nerve-racking."

"Good job. You kept really, really cool there." When I slumped back in my chair, Rit came out with a cup for me. "Here, my special tea."

"Ahhh, that's a nice smell."

It was brewed using quality tea leaves, and Rit had added a spoonful of mead, too. The taste reminded me of drinking mead with Rit, a relaxing memory.

"All right, so the situation's improved, but what now?" Tisse asked.

I set the cup on the table and considered the question for a moment.

"About that… I'd like us to work on convincing Lavender, so our efforts should be focused on supporting Rit."

"What about Van? Is it okay to leave him be?"

"I'll do what I can with him…but I doubt I'll get many opportunities."

Van was unsure because he didn't know how to interpret the Guide blessing in relation to his Hero blessing. My best guess was that he'd decide on an answer after the third time I spoke with him. The Hero recovered from any doubt brought on by sudden shock, and it never took that long.

"This was my first talk, so now I've only got two more to get through to him. What to do…? I'll need to come up with something quickly."

"This can't be easy if it's forcing you to use a more rash tactic," Tisse remarked.

Rit hummed. "I'd like to believe convincing Lavender will get us closer to what we want, but…I should think things over a bit more."

I took another sip of tea.

Danan sighed and scratched the back of his head. "Hahhh, what a pain. I could do with an enemy who just needs their ass kicked."

"We can't deal with things here like we did when fighting the demon lord's army... Although I confess, I feel the same," Yarandrala said. She and Danan shared a laugh.

Yeah, I'm starting to miss when things were simple enough to resolve with just a fight, too.

Chapter 4

Confusion and Then Rampage

You never know what life will throw at you.

Sure, things had causes, but recognizing them in advance was beyond mortal capability.

I guess what I'm getting at is…we ran into a problem.

"I'm really sorry to bother you when you're busy."

Five days after Van's party came to the shop, Megria, the Adventurers Guild receptionist, came by the store. She stared at her shoes apologetically as she stood there in her uniform.

Yarandrala, Danan, Tisse, Rit, and I were there. Ruti was working at the plantation.

"We'd really appreciate it if Ms. Ruti and Ms. Tisse would take on a quest to handle some seabogeys discovered on the coast…"

"I see. You certainly can't let that problem sit."

Seabogeys were devilish things that came from the ocean. They resembled male humans wearing hats, but what appeared to be their heads were actually camouflage. Their real faces were on their stomachs. Seabogeys radiated an aura of terror that manipulated minds, and they stole life essence from terrified victims to strengthen themselves.

Dealing with them without a way to resist their influence was extremely difficult, making the monsters dangerous for weak adventurers, even a mob of them.

That's why seabogeys were known as low-level killers.

The creatures could threaten entire settlements. Seabogeys were a variant of bogeymen, monsters that ate children, meaning they weren't the sort to raze villages, but their inclinations were hardly preferable.

There was no logic to it. It was difficult to find a biological reason for why they consumed kids. Whatever the explanation, seabogeys only stuffed human children into the big, black mouths that split open their torsos. It was as if they were born from malice and meant to torture humans specifically.

For all that, an experienced bunch of C rankers should have been able to handle them.

"Everyone is out on quests, so there's no one left who can go right now."

In an unexpected way, Van had caused this.

He'd spread a lot of money around hiring people to move the beached *Vendidad*. And thanks to that shift in the economy, lots of organizations had had the capital to file a bunch of quests to handle issues they'd been putting off. Zoltan's more talented adventurers had taken all those jobs and were presently away from the town.

Plus, Van's leveling had wiped out the monsters at the top of the food chain in the south seas, which was likely what had caused the seabogeys to migrate.

Undoubtedly, that hadn't been Van's intention, but that's how things had shaken out.

"I understand someone needs to take the quest, but…"

The problem was who would go.

Any of us could handle it alone. But considering Van's presence, I didn't want to be away from Zoltan for long. Rit and I were needed to negotiate with Lavender and Van. Yarandrala's ability to control plants was necessary for keeping tabs on the Hero's party. Tisse maintained lines of retreat in the event of a fight and kept in contact with Esta. Danan was our strongest fighter, so even if he didn't have anything to do at present, he needed to be ready at a moment's notice. And we couldn't let Ruti do anything to draw attention. Van finding her was the worst-case scenario.

In which case...

I glanced at the spider on Tisse's shoulder. Mister Crawly Wawly hopped up as if to say, "Leave it to me."

"No, that's a little too..."

He was a reliable spider, and he'd probably be able to endure the seabogeys' terror aura, but a swarm of the monsters posed a threat to a lone C-rank adventurer.

But Mister Crawly Wawly might just be able to...

"A group of goblins would be one thing, but Mister Crawly Wawly can't handle a bunch of seabogeys," Tisse stated.

Mister Crawly Wawly slumped dejectedly.

So he can *beat a group of goblins, huh?*

"The only option is for me to handle this swiftly," Tisse added, volunteering herself.

Her leaving was worrisome, but with things more or less settled with Van for the moment, letting Tisse go was probably the best choice...

"Wait..." I reviewed an idea that popped into my head.

Will that work?

"I think Rit, Danan, and I should take this quest."

"Rit the hero is going?!" Megria exclaimed.

"Yeah, this is a special exception," I replied.

"Thank you so much! Thank goodness!"

Megria smiled, sighing with relief before leaving with a polite bow.

"Sorry for deciding that without asking, but would the two of you give me a hand?"

"Of course. It'll be nice to cut loose, even if it's against some chaff monsters," Danan said.

"I've got no complaints, but what about Van?" Rit's question was understandable.

I took a deep breath. "The truth is, I think we should invite Van and fight these monsters with him."

""What?!""

"Are you serious? You're telling me I have to work with that asshole?!"

"You only have two more chances at negotiating with Van, right? Is it really okay to use one for this?"

"And Van will prioritize killing monsters and raising his level over saving people. Who knows what sort of problem that might cause?"

Danan, Yarandrala, and Tisse were all clearly concerned.

"What do you think, Rit?" I inquired.

She'd been deep in thought from the moment I'd raised the idea.

"Hmmm... I've been talking with Lavender every day since the meeting in the shop. It feels like I'm just one push away, but I need some kind of opening... Showing her the relationship I have with Red will reach her better than words."

"Do you think you can get Lavender to agree to come hunt seabogeys with us?" I asked.

"If Van says he'll go, Lavender will come. And I don't think she'll get in the way of the job itself."

"But she will try to stop me from talking to Van, I guess."

"Yeah. I hoped to get her to promise not to interfere with that, but I haven't made much progress with her on that front."

"Oh well. Van and Lavender are difficult people, so this was never going to be easy. We'll just have to do our best to get the quest done."

If conversation alone wasn't enough to convince the Hero, then there was no choice but to change the setting to create an opening.

This promised to be another ad-lib negotiation.

"If the two mediators are fine with it, then I'm not gonna object. And you're gonna bring me along, too, in case anything happens, right? I don't like the idea of working with that jerk, but I'll suck it up." Danan grinned.

He always knew his best course of action. Knowing we had the ultimate Martial Artist on our side was part of why I felt confident using such a bold tactic.

"We'll need to stay on guard against Van while fighting monsters. I'll be counting on you," I said.

Danan nodded. "Just leave it to me."

Okay. Our enemy is a swarm of dangerous monsters, so we'd best prepare.

*   *   *

Two hours later, on the road headed south.

"Get along now, move it!"

The stable boy gripping the reins called out, but the donkey pulling the cart didn't even pretend to make an effort as it slowly trudged along the narrow road. The cart was loaded with fish and coconuts.

This trail linked Zoltan with a fishing village on the coast. Unlike the western road, which led toward the continent's center, this path was narrow and poorly maintained. It only consisted of gravel; there was no stone paving.

"Clearing the way for that dingy cart? You're too nice, Van!" Lavender said when the Hero stepped into a puddle to move aside for the donkey-drawn wagon.

If the choice was between moving a cart or moving a few people, the answer was obvious. It wasn't about being kind, it was merely basic judgment.

Lavender would never accept that sort of reasoning, though, so I didn't waste my breath.

"We'll be there soon; you should get ready to fight."

"I'm always ready. The Hero is ever-prepared to fight."

Van responded to my warning with a cheerful tone. His voice didn't sound like that of someone about to enter combat, but that was Van the Hero for you. To him, battle wasn't something that required changing to a special mindset; it was his normal.

Blessing impulses didn't care what sort of situation the person was in, so perhaps God wanted people to be like Van. However, I preferred how Ruti was a little more careless when we weren't in a fight.

Those imperfections were how Ruti the Hero's personality shone through. That was all she'd had before she was freed from her blessing. Did that mean this was the real Van?

A Hero who was 100 percent subservient to the Hero's urges?

Powerful impulses wouldn't affect someone never at odds with their blessing. However, I didn't really know Van as a person well enough to understand who he had been before his blessing awakened.

"I see them," Van announced.

A line of dark figures walked along the beach, an ominous procession of tall, hunched-over bodies. Their legs dragged as they trudged through the sand.

"The seabogeys."

"So you and I will fight up front, right, Gideon?"

"Yeah, Rit and Lavender will support us with magic, and Danan can take care of any that try to escape. Letting any get away will be bad."

"I'd rather let loose and go wild a bit, but if that's what I'm supposed to do, then you can count on me."

There was no need to worry about missing one with Danan on cleanup, leaving us free to focus on the immediate threats.

I needed to land some shots on Van's worldview while also taking care of the monsters. Danan would be crucial if this turned into a fight with Van and Lavender, but he was also here so I could focus on speaking with Van.

I drew my weapon.

"Why a bronze sword?" Van questioned.

His sword was a replica of Ruti's Holy Demon Slayer. It had been crafted only recently, so it lacked history, but its blade was as keen as any legendary ancient weapon's.

My bronze sword couldn't begin to compare.

"When I left the party, I returned my gear. I didn't need it since I was withdrawing from the battle to save the world."

"But even so, we all have to fight so long as we live, don't we?"

"That's true. Which is why I carry this bronze sword."

"Ummm..."

Van looked like he sort of understood, yet also didn't.

Unlike his exchanges with Esta, this was a discussion about a blessing other than that of the Hero. Van had absolute confidence when it came to his blessing, but there were many things he didn't understand about other people's. His belief in remaining obedient to Divine Blessings meant he couldn't comment on other people acting in accordance with theirs.

So it should be more effective talking to him about the Guide than about the Hero.

"Okay, I'll take the right, you handle the left, Van."

"Yes, sir!"

We started running, tearing into the seabogey swarm from both sides.

""Wah-hah-hah-hah-hah.""

The seabogeys made a sound like human laughter. The eerie voices didn't possess a magical effect, but they'd terrify any normal villagers who tried to exterminate the monsters.

And fear gave the seabogeys strength.

"With his blessing, Van won't feel scared, so no need to worry there."

The seabogeys were more intelligent than most creatures, but not as clever as people. Ordinarily, they didn't employ high-level tactics in battle.

"Phantom Pain."

"Circle of Fear."

"Horror."

They cast a sequence of psychic magic.

Seabogeys tended to possess the Sorcerer blessing more than most others. Around one in three had it, enabling them to wield a variety of spells. In particular, they favored magic that afflicted the mind to induce fear or agony.

They used those spells outside of battle, too—on the children they kidnapped.

According to a monster scholar, seabogeys enjoyed eating children more when their victims were crying in pain and terror. It just went to show that there were evil monsters in this world that had to be slain and could not be tolerated peacefully.

"Spirit of spring, blow the horn of snowmelt! Sowing Horn!"

A trumpeting sound echoed across the beach. Rit had cast some spirit magic to raise morale and counter fear. Because seabogeys converted terror into energy, the spell also caused them to falter.

"The Phantom Pain will linger, but that much won't be a problem."

"This sort of magic is useless against the Hero!"

Phantom Pain was a subtle spell that dulled one's movements by inflicting an illusory ache. It felt like being pricked with a needle, but it didn't cause a physical wound.

""Hahhh!""

""Wah-hah! Hah-hah! Wah-hah-hah!""

The seabogeys went down in droves, all while laughing eerily.

"These aren't difficult opponents, but the Hero shall defeat any evil!"

That was the Hero for you.

The seabogeys slashed at Van with their claws, but he cut the monsters down one after the other, each one felled by a precise strike to a vital point.

The Enhanced Critical Hits and Advanced Weapon Proficiency skills, huh?

One made vitals visible, even on nonhumanoid opponents, and the other made Van's blade accurate enough to hit those targets. While each attack was swift, precise, and powerful, there was no intent behind them. Van's sword gave the impression that its wielder was merely repeating a set motion. There was no spirit in any of it, no actual desire to slay the enemy.

"So that's it."

Some warriors could lose themselves in their bladework, but this was something different. Van's motions were mechanical.

A sword brandished by a blessing, I guess you could call it.

"Wah-hah-hah."

"Whoa there, I'm not going to let you get a hit."

I dodged a seabogey's claws and then cut it down with a single counterstrike. I followed up by slashing the one behind me, then backed off a step to avoid the claws of a seabogey that stepped over the first one's corpse, finally attacking it when it was off-balance.

Meanwhile, Van was…

Hmmm…

I assumed a low stance with my sword and then ran forward.

"…!"

A seabogey had bitten Van's left arm. But his expression remained completely unchanged as he stabbed it. It was a lethal blow, but it left a slight opening while he pulled his blade free. A deep thrust was a poor choice of attack when one was dealing with a large number of enemies.

The group of seabogeys around Van charged in when he stopped moving, and I leaped to his side, cutting down three of the monsters in quick succession.

"You don't need to worry about me, Gideon."

"I see that you fight with the intent to use Healing Hands later. Is that because you don't defend or can't defend?"

"I just battle at full strength, no matter the enemy!"

We stood back-to-back while dealing with the seabogeys trying to surround us.

"Against inferior opponents, you shouldn't fight in a way that assumes taking damage!"

Our swords both flashed, and seabogey blood stained the sand.

"Never hold back when facing evil! That is how the Hero battles!"

"Holding back is something reserved for taking it easy. It's not the same as adapting your tactics to suit the opponent."

Only ten seabogeys remained from the initial horde.

"How many did you kill?" I questioned.

"Huh?"

"You don't even know how many you've felled?"

"Is there a reason to keep track?" Van cocked his head in confusion. "The Hero must defeat wickedness. Be it one, one thousand, or one million enemies, I will keep fighting so long as evil persists."

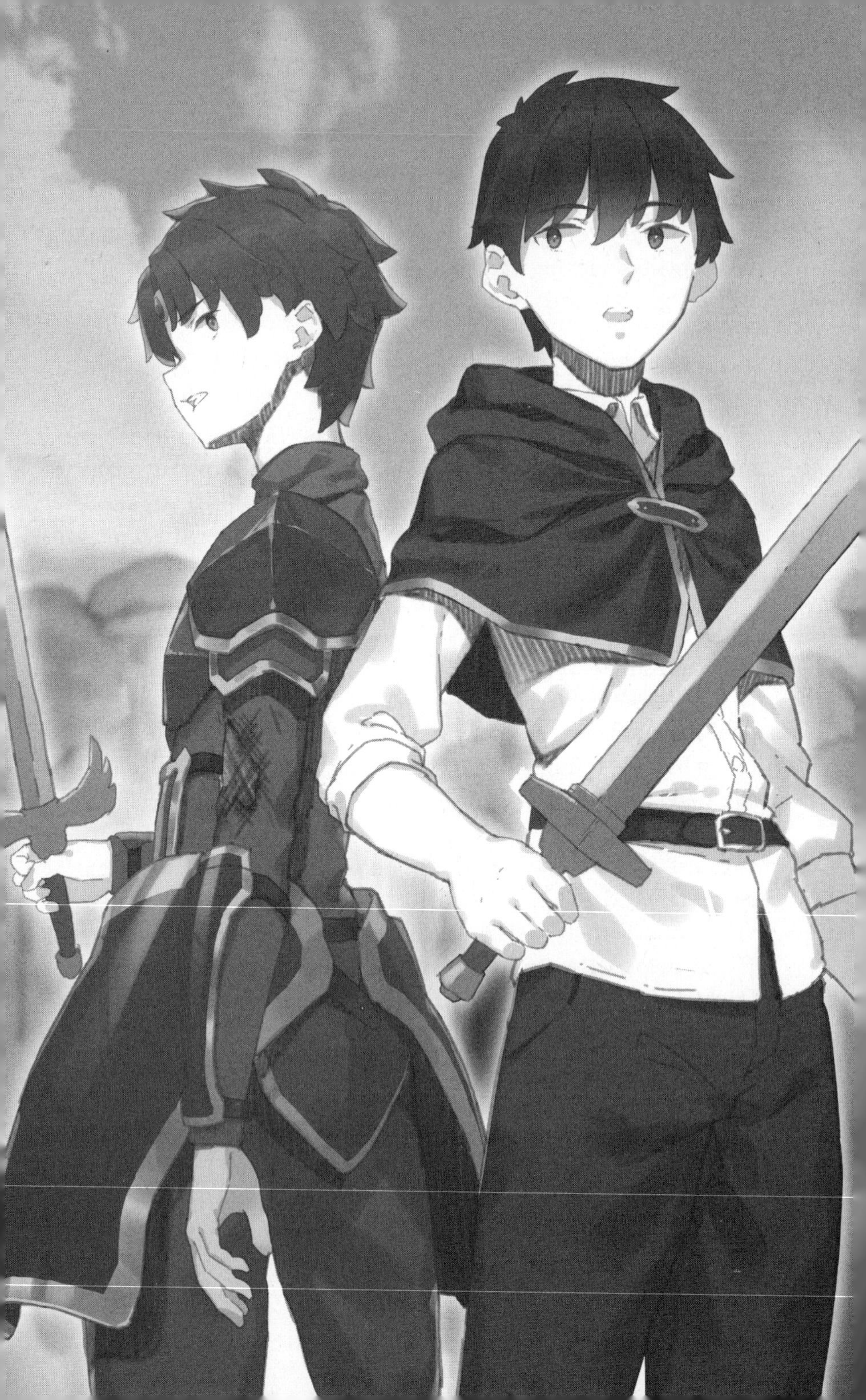

"You're weak, Van."

"I do not desire strength. God made the Hero to be the mightiest blessing, and I intend to raise my level and become more powerful than anyone."

"There were forty-five seabogeys at the start. I took care of twenty-four, you got seventeen, Danan two, and Rit one."

"...What of it?"

Van finished the last of the seabogeys.

That's the quest complete.

"Who defeated the most enemies is a simple method for determining who had the most important role in battle. Despite the Hero blessing's incredible power, you slew fewer seabogeys than I did."

"That's..."

"If you think the Hero is a special blessing, then you'll need to work to rectify that disparity."

Van sheathed his blade and fell silent.

Esta wouldn't say something like this to him.

The Hero meant too much to Esta, perhaps because she'd met Ruti only after she'd grown strong. However, I had known Ruti before she was powerful. My sister hadn't always been effortlessly strong. She'd worked hard for that might.

In that sense, Van, who relied on the power of his blessing, was weaker than Ruti. His sword paid no mind to what manner of enemy stood against it, preferring to assert its strength. Van was able to fight so recklessly because of Healing Hands, the Hero's unique skill. Yet if he ever encountered a situation where Healing Hands wasn't enough, it would be the end for him.

Simply telling him that wasn't enough, though. His absolute faith in blessings would keep him from accepting it. He believed that the strength given by blessings was everything. If he lost despite relying on that, then it was just God's will.

Instead, I tried using myself as a comparison.

"The Guide is a blessing to lead the Hero. You could say that the

Hero isn't complete until they can surpass me in every way. That's what I think, at least. What do you think, Van?"

"...Mm, I believe you may be right."

His ideology left him unable to deny the relationship between the Hero and the Guide. For the first time in a long while, perhaps ever, Van considered how he'd been fighting.

"Van!!!"

Whoops, looks like someone's here to get in the way.

Lavender came zooming in, clinging to Van's cheek while glaring venomously at me. Her eyes were filled with murder. If Rit hadn't been there, it might have actually become a fight.

"I was just stating the facts." I shrugged with a smile.

Had I been discussing philosophies, Lavender would have openly rejected me right away, but she couldn't deny reality.

This fairy is wiser than I thought.

From her look, I gleaned that she understood the problems with Van's fighting. She recognized his weaknesses, yet was fine with how the boy was. A lover so willing to accept anything and everything could ruin someone.

"What?" Lavender demanded, perhaps noticing my attention lingering on her.

"Nothing, nothing," I replied. "More importantly, I didn't see you giving much support."

"I did too!"

Lavender had used a couple of spells, like Tailwind, to support Van's movement and Thunder Stomp to send a shock wave through the ground and topple an enemy for Van. However, each bit of magic had been elementary, hardly the limit for someone who put Danan and Rit on guard.

"Your timing was great, and you were really helpful, Lavender."

"Awww, thank you, Van!" She kissed Van's cheek.

Lavender's nature leaned heavily toward destruction; she had to be better suited to damaging spells than support magic.

But she doesn't want Van to see her that way.

She'd used magic against Rit and Danan, so clearly, she wasn't concerned with concealing her strength from people at large. Perhaps if she called upon destructive spells too often, she'd be unable to maintain her present form.

That was the extent of my understanding of Lavender and Van.

I'd like to talk with Rit and form a plan.

Just then, Rit, who'd been staring out at the beach, shouted, "Red! There's one seabogey left!"

"What?!" I exclaimed.

Van and I dashed over to Rit.

"What did you find?" I asked.

Rit motioned with her hand. "Do you see these tracks?"

"They're from a little earlier, before the battle."

"Yeah, and they lead this way before departing."

"There's a village not far in that direction."

"So one of them went to the village, but it came back, right?"

Rit nodded at Van's question.

"Right, one of them went to the village, returned here to gather its friends, and then started back the way it came—"

"To take a child." There was a change in Van's expression… He was furious.

"Most likely, a child has already been taken. Upon seeing as much, the other seabogeys would have set out for the village."

"Then we have to go help them at once!"

Van believed that whether an individual lived or died was the will of God, but children were an exception that needed protecting.

Every creature was supposed to live and die in accordance with the role set for them by their blessing. However, most kids hadn't connected with their blessings yet. Without knowing one's role, it was impossible to live by it, so children needed to be kept safe. That was a fundamental teaching of the church.

If a child unaware of their blessing was slain, it didn't feed the killer's blessing. If Demis's will was killing to advance one's blessing, then harming children, who couldn't contribute to another's blessing level, was the worst possible crime.

Actually, that wasn't written anywhere explicitly, but every theologian who studied scripture agreed about that interpretation.

That dogma was part of why the church managed orphanages worldwide.

Kids were to be safeguarded; even Van agreed on that.

"We need to move..." I turned to Van. "Can you follow the tracks?"

"I can't..."

There was an unsteadiness in his voice.

He only took skills best suited to fighting. It was a natural choice, considering the Hero's role and the church's teachings, which valued fighting and developing one's blessing.

"Got it. Rit and I will handle this."

"Okay..." Van's shoulders slumped.

"The Hero shouldn't look like that." I patted his back with a smile. "The Hero is always a symbol of hope. Just be glad that Rit and I can read the footprints. You can think on this more when the danger's past."

"Right."

Van didn't have much experience with this form of adventuring. Maybe that was the result of the warped Hero he'd created for himself.

"...I've got a bit of a bad feeling about this," I muttered.

"Huh?"

"No, it's nothing."

There was something about the Hero's impulses and Van's personality that didn't quite line up.

I had seen Ruti's earliest days with the Hero blessing. Naturally, her kind and adorable personality hadn't been created by the Hero's impulses, but still, it felt odd that this second Hero blessing would come to someone with Van's disposition.

"Hey, Van." Lavender tugged at his ear.

"What is it?"

"You just need to find a creature shaped like one of them, right?"

"You mean like a seabogey?"

"Mhm. I can find it."

"Really?!"

"Of course. I'd never lie to you, Van!"

Lavender's eyes sparkled. Clearly, she was overjoyed to be useful to Van. Perhaps she'd been frustrated that Rit had offered more support during the fight.

"Amazing. You can locate a seabogey from far away?"

"Yup. I know every living creature the wind touches," she responded confidently.

So that's it. She senses things using the wind.

The way Lavender spoke suggested she could differentiate between humans and seabogeys on a general level, but needed to know an individual's specific shape to recognize them.

Having an archfay-level fairy as a comrade isn't fair. That would have been so convenient on our journey...

"Okay, Van...and the rest of you! Follow me!"

"Yeah, let's go help as fast as we can!"

Van ran off after Lavender, who flew through the air.

The rest of us hurried along behind the Hero and his fairy.

"Hey, Red." Danan, who'd kept silent until now, came up beside me and whispered in my ear. "Now we know what Lavender can do. Seems like something we can deal with, too."

"Yeah."

"How far ahead have you got this all plotted out? Damn, I'm gettin' flashbacks to your Gideon days."

"I'm hoping this'll just be a one-time thing..."

Honestly, I already wanted to stop with these tense negotiations. We had to do the best we could for the kidnapped child, though. I'd discussed the possibility of a kid being taken beforehand with Rit and had asked her to investigate the tracks once the fighting was over.

Using an abduction as an opening to further my agenda with Van was rough on my heart now that I was Red.

"When this is over, let's relax in the bath together."

"Rit... Yeah, I'd like to take it easy a bit."

Just a little more effort to ensure our slow life is safe.

*   *   *

At best, our odds were fifty-fifty that the kid was still alive.

It all hinged on whether the seabogey had decided to eat the child immediately or wring more terror out of them.

"Boo...hoo..."

From the depths of an ocean-carved cave, there was a faint, hoarse voice mixing with the sounds of the waves.

Ordinary people wouldn't have been familiar with the noise, but none of us were ordinary.

All right.

I gave the signal and looked at Van to tell him to move in.

"Van...!"

Unfortunately, he leaped forward before I gave the word. His hand reached for his sword hilt as he charged into the dark.

"He doesn't have the Night Vision skill! Lavender!"

"I know! Don't give me orders!"

Lavender immediately cast a spell.

"Wisp!"

An orb of light as bright as a lantern flew off after Van.

We hurriedly gave chase.

""Wah-hah-hah.""

There were two seabogeys. Van was charging at one, and the other hid in the shadow of a boulder. Normally, he would have noticed it, but it was dark, and he was distracted by anger.

Van's sword cleaved the first seabogey in half. And that's when the second lunged at his back with fangs bared.

"Wah-hah...?!"

"Van! I told you not to fight assuming you'll be wounded!"

I hurled my sword to pierce the seabogey's torso through.

"Wah-hah-hah..."

With a final eerie laugh, the monster collapsed.

"Damn you!" Van thrust his sword into the seabogey to finish it off.

"Is the child safe?" I asked.

"Here!" Van rushed over to a little girl lying on the ground.

"This is horrible!" Rit gasped when she saw the girl illuminated by the magic light.

The poor child had been tortured, physically and mentally. Shock blinded her to our presence. Her voice was hoarse; all she could manage was a painful, rasping breath.

"We can keep her alive, but my magic can't fully…" Rit's voice was tight.

"It's okay. Van's here," I said.

Van stowed his sword and placed his right hand on the girl's forehead.

"Healing Hands!" Van's body shone brightly.

The same skill could differ depending on the user. Ruti's Healing Hands had a warm, gentle glow, but Van's was an intense gleam that stirred up life force.

"Ah… Ah…"

With her injuries mended, the girl suddenly found her voice.

"Waaaaaaaaaah!!!!" She cried as though to make up for all the tears she'd forgotten before, and she clung to Van's chest.

The Hero looked unsure of what to do, and he could only manage to let the girl sob while rubbing her back like a parent.

* * *

"Thank you very much! I don't know how we can possibly repay you!"

The girl's parents thanked us repeatedly.

"It's fine. We accepted a quest from the guild to slay the monsters. Helping her was just part of our job," I replied, watching Van's expression out of the corner of my eye all the while.

"It's the Hero's duty to save people. I don't require gratitude."

"Sir Hero… Lord Demis, thank you for sending the Hero to us!"

He brushed the parents off, as he did with all the people he helped. This time, however, that coldness came off as humility to the parents, which only strengthened their reverence for him.

"Sir Hero," the girl squeaked through her raw throat, looking up at Van. "Thank you."

"...No problem," Van answered gruffly, but he appeared far more human at that moment than I'd ever seen him.

* * *

The next day, we gathered at a restaurant in the harbor district.

"Van what? That's...a rather sudden change. It's difficult to believe." Esta sounded impressed as she ate her squid ink pasta.

Not that it meant much, but I couldn't imagine her eating squid ink pasta back when she was Theodora.

Maybe that's just my imagination, though.

"Mmm, that's delicious."

She eagerly twirled another large bite onto her fork.

Beside her, Albert ate with similar gusto.

"Rit should have come, too. The pasta here is great."

"She and Danan are talking with Lavender right now."

"It's amazing that you actually spoke with Van, but it's just as impressive that Rit's gotten Lavender to open up."

"She's using love as a common base to build on. Lavender apparently noticed she and Van weren't as coordinated in battle as Rit and me. That's what they're discussing now."

For Van and Lavender, the bottleneck was their limited worldviews—Divine Blessings for Van and love for Lavender. Our goal was to convince them there was value in things beyond those narrow fields.

Esta set her fork down. "It never seems to work."

"Hmm? What?"

"Just talking about myself. I've had plenty of opportunities to speak with Van and Lavender on our travels. I never made an impact on their opinions, yet you both got through to them so quickly. It's a bit of a strike to the ego."

So she's feeling a bit down about herself, huh?

I hadn't noticed while we adventured together, but Esta bottled up her discontent and was quick to blame herself for any troubles. She'd cited her own lack of strength when Ruti wasn't getting the help she needed, and she'd done the same when issues in our party pushed us to the verge of dissolving the group.

Esta was an excellent warrior and cleric, but she had a habit of trying to resolve everything alone.

I wanted to say something tactful to lift her spirits, but I was coming up short.

"But the current developments are all thanks to you, Lady Esta."

Before I thought up a reply, Albert chimed in.

"You think?"

"Yes, you were the one who sent me ahead to warn everyone about Van. Without that decision, our situation would be very different. I think you should have a little confidence in what you've achieved."

"H-hmm. I suppose…you're right."

"Red, Rit, and the others are taking care of things that you can't handle, and the situation is far better than the worst case we feared."

Not bad, Albert.

"I—I see…"

"Please, don't put yourself down. You hide behind a mask and downplay your accomplishments, but I know the lengths you've gone to for us to reach this point."

Albert's hero worship has undergone an interesting change.

"You two make a good combo." The remark came almost unconsciously. I couldn't help myself.

Esta's cheeks flushed. "D-don't be silly! W-wait. I didn't mean it like that. He's a perfectly suitable partner. Ah, don't look at me like that, Albert!"

This was going to give me heartburn.

"You're the one person I don't want to hear that from, Red!" At some point, Esta had grown angry with me.

"Anyway..." Albert pursed his lips. "If love is the key for getting through to Lavender, then it's no wonder it was difficult for Lady Esta."

"Mrgh, even I..."

"For someone of her level, most men are probably no better than a stone on the road, and she doesn't have time to think much about love since she's so busy guiding the Hero. Lavender just isn't the sort of problem she can deal with."

This guy... He's really taken his blockheadedness to a new level. He's even developed a knack for speaking up at the worst moment.

At the very least, Esta seemed to calm down a bit.

"Shall we return to a more serious topic?"

"Yeah."

Her voice was clearly more subdued, but Albert didn't appear to notice.

"Looks like rough seas ahead. Good luck."

"I didn't ask you. But when this is all over, I'm coming to you for some advice."

I'd never imagined I'd have this conversation with Esta. Before I knew it, I was laughing.

"Sheesh. We should be discussing Zoltan's lack of adventurers, not playing around..." Esta wore a troubled look as she chided me, but there was a bit of happiness in her eyes.

"All right. So Albert will handle the jobs that have piled up?" I said.

Esta nodded. "Yes."

"Will you two be okay splitting up? He's been helping you with a bunch of things, hasn't he?"

"I won't be spending every waking moment on quests. I know Zoltan's adventurers. I've distributed quests based on suitability and have been supporting parties on their assignments. If there's anything a group can't handle, I'll deal with it myself."

I cocked an eyebrow. "Oh? I'm surprised the Adventurers Guild is so willing to cooperate."

"Indeed. I'm sure those in charge aren't happy letting a man who betrayed Zoltan manage things, but…their desire not to rely on Van is evidently greater."

"He really is despised."

"His plan to brainwash everyone was kept quiet, but people know how poorly he treated the mayor and the other higher-ups, and that he brought the dragons." Albert shrugged. "It just means they'd rather have my help than Van's. Well, and my help is free."

Albert had been granted amnesty for his crimes during the Devil's Blessing incident in exchange for rendering services to the church for atonement. He was denied any pay except for charitable donations.

"There's no denying my role in bringing harm to Zoltan, so I'm glad to be of use now."

Bighawk and Albert had fanned the flames to get people living in the slum of Southmarsh to attempt a coup.

Albert had intended to turn Zoltan into a military dictatorship and lead an army to join the Hero's party.

How ironic that now he was protecting Zoltan from the Hero.

You never know what's going to happen in life.

"My efforts should keep emergency quests from falling in your lap, so you can focus on dealing with Van."

"That's a big help. I managed to turn the seabogey trouble into a lesson for Van, but I've likely only got one more shot to get through to him," I said.

"From what I've heard, it seems like the things he saw on that quest shook him substantially."

"Unfortunately, the pillar of his faith is rock solid, and the logic based on the scripture is sturdy. The holy church is an organization greater than any country on this continent. Its philosophy is nothing to make light of," I replied.

Theologians as far back as the earliest historical records had constructed the church's ideologies to shift with the times and deal with heretics who turned their efforts against the church's authority.

The beliefs Van had been immersed in while studying in the

monastery, combined with the Hero's mental fortitude, would surely straighten out his doubts before long.

I have to settle this with the next meeting.

"I have to make the final blow soon."

This was a siege, and the stronghold was on the verge of collapse. However, there was a limit to my side's supplies. Should the next attack fail, there would be a counterattack that would leave things in a dangerous spot.

"Ugh. This really is bad for the heart," I groused.

"Wasn't this normal back in the old days?" Esta remarked.

Back then, failure had meant the end. We'd come up against do-or-die scenarios while fighting the demon lord's army all the time.

"Thinking back on it now, I really did some crazy stuff." I'd never admitted to it, but there had been plenty of times when I'd lost hope. When we exited the bewitching woods only to see the demon lord's army amassed before us, I was prepared to die.

"Rit told me how your eyes shone with confidence during the trouble in Loggervia, and how you said you never attempted things you couldn't do."

"I just said I was confident the distraction would work. Admitting I thought I might die would have weighed on Rit…and Ares."

"…True." After mention of that name, Esta shook her head and changed topics. "I will keep on as I have been, working with Ljubo to convince Van. I haven't noticed much change in Van, but Lavender's counterarguments have grown weaker lately. I guess that's the result of Rit's efforts."

"If we can get Lavender onto our side on this, do you think we have a chance?" I asked.

"Is that what you're aiming for, Red?"

"Yeah, that would be best, but…"

"But?"

"Life can be strange. You never know what will happen."

"Indeed…"

Chapter 4: Confusion and Then Rampage

At the very least, I knew I had to make preparations to protect our lives here.

*   *   *

"Welcome back, Big Brother."

Ruti greeted me from behind the counter when I returned to the shop.

"Thanks, Ruti. Is Rit not back yet?"

"Not yet."

There's still plenty of medicine on the shelves. After all the recent restocking, we should be fine for a little while.

"I'm going to stick around the store for a bit. What about you? Going to go back to the plantation?"

"No, I finished the work there this morning."

"Ah. I'll make sure there's enough dinner for you, too, then."

"Hooray." Ruti lifted her arms and cheered, a heartwarming display. I stood next to her behind the counter.

"Shall we handle the customers together?"

"Mhm."

There weren't many visitors today, just a few looking for common medicines.

"You won't believe this, Red! Albert chose us for a quest!"

"We ordinarily wouldn't take this kind of job, but he said we'd be fine as long as we had a Poison Resistance potion."

A D-rank party in high spirits stopped in for a quick purchase. They were the first group in a stream of adventurers.

"Red! I need a bottle of cure potion!"

"Thunder Enchantment oil!"

"Three alkali bottles! Apparently, those will make it easy to deal with pseudodragon slimes."

Evidently, Albert was giving advice to the parties he assigned on quests. As a result, we were selling a lot of the more expensive potions for adventuring, which was good for business.

He always did have the potential to be Zoltan's hero.

The man seemed satisfied with his current place, but I wondered what he might have looked like holding his head high with pride as Zoltan's number one.

"'Thanks for the purchase.'"

Evening arrived quickly.

The rush of customers on their way home from work died down, leaving a bit of free time before closing.

"I should take care of the cleaning now." I stepped away from the counter to get the mop ready.

"Big Brother."

"What is it?"

"...Are you okay?" Ruti eyed me with concern.

"Hah-hah. You can tell, huh?"

"Mhm. You're really tired."

Van was a powerful enemy in more ways than raw strength. The church's backing was his most dangerous quality.

"The cleaning."

"Hmm? Ah, yeah, I was getting to that."

"No, let's do it together," Ruti said, taking the cleaning supplies from the back. "It's faster with two people. And more fun."

"I suppose so."

The two of us got to work.

"Go from front to rear."

We began by wiping away dust.

"You've really gotten pretty good at tidying the store," I remarked.

"Because I've helped out so many times."

During the winter, before Ruti moved to the plantation, she'd assisted around the shop a lot. She'd picked up how to work at an apothecary back then, too, so there was no problem with leaving her to watch the place alone. Similarly, she knew how to clean up.

After dusting came sweeping, gathering up the trash with the broom before disposing of it.

"I'll get the water."

"And I'll throw away the garbage."

We divided up the tasks and finished by mopping the floors.

"It's shiny clean."

"It goes quickly with the two of us, and it's easier to do a better job."

No other customers came by that day. A nice little break like that was welcome on occasion. It allowed me to enjoy a pleasant moment with Ruti.

"I'm back."

"Hey! I'm here to eat."

Danan came back with Rit.

Dinner for four, then?

"All right, shall I make something a bit fancier?"

"Oh? What have you got in mind?" Rit asked happily.

"Diced steak and dried shellfish grilled in butter, a tomato and cheese salad, cream soup, and an apple tart for dessert."

"Ohhh! Sounds great! But that sounds like a lot of work."

I hadn't prepared anything, and starting from scratch would take a while.

"Let me help. I can prepare the ingredients."

"Yeah, I'll pitch in, too! I can get the oven warm with my magic."

"Then I'll go out and buy whatever you're missing."

Ruti, Rit, and Danan all offered to help.

"I know you like cooking for us, but sometimes we want to assist when you're tired," Rit said.

"Thanks, I appreciate it."

We all shared a smile.

Yeah, today's a good day.

※　　　　　※　　　　　※

The next day, at Zoltan's Adventurers Guild, Albert read over the quest sheet in his hand.

"A child has been missing since yesterday. Not a lot of information, but there are no signs of dangerous monsters. Did she just get lost in the woods, or was she kidnapped by goblins, or...? A D-rank party could handle this, but..."

Albert scanned the map, double-checking the area around the village where the client lived.

"A farming village near the river mouth. It provides grain and such to the fishing settlements near the sea... The problem is, that's pretty close to where the seabogeys showed up."

The seabogeys ought to be dead, but there was no guarantee none had survived. And sending a half-baked party of adventurers against seabogeys was a recipe for disaster.

"But considering the reward, I can't assign a skilled party."

Albert considered the worst possible scenario. An abduction did no major harm to the whole village. The client was the girl's father—a farmer—and the reward was the meager sum he could muster. It was only enough to hire a low-tier D-rank party or a solo adventurer.

"Guess I have to take this one."

Judging that it was best if he dealt with it, Albert took action.

* * *

Albert cut a different figure from his old, heroic one.

Now he sported only practical armor with no excessive ornaments. His sword was sharp, but not showy, and the weapon was one-handed, so he could wield it. Although Albert's prosthetic hand was of an exquisite design, not immediately recognizable as false, and able to grip basic tools, it wasn't strong enough to brandish a weapon.

Unlike Danan, who was a veritable monster of martial arts, Albert couldn't continue practicing the same combat style he'd employed with both hands. Still, his blessing level had gone up from all the battles he'd fought alongside Esta during their travels. He'd managed to develop fighting strength equal to, or possibly even greater than, that of the man he used to be.

"A pair of ogres, huh?"

Albert stood before the two monsters in the woods. Each held a tree trunk like a club in its thick arms.

"Hmph." Albert drew his sword with his left hand. "If this is all, then I really could have sent someone else."

"Guoooo!!!"

He dashed in as one of the ogres howled furiously. It swung its club at the small creature that dared to run at it. However, the little thing did not have its skull cracked and brain splattered; it raced past the ogre's attack.

"Guo?!"

The second one frantically swung its club.

"Too late!"

Albert disappeared, and the second ogre's club slammed into the first's chest.

The first ogre was wobbly from the blow, while the second was agitated over striking its partner. And while they were distracted, a blade flashed twice.

""Guooooo?!""

The fight was over.

The pair of monsters collapsed and stopped breathing while Albert cleaned his sword.

"Now, about the child."

He sheathed his blade and looked around. He sensed something nearby and approached it cautiously, ready to draw at any moment.

"Roar!"

There was a shrill voice, and a small dragon with butterfly wings flew out of the undergrowth and pounced on Albert.

"Mrgh!"

He reflexively swatted it down.

"Kyuuuu..."

"Ah, apologies. That was a reflex." Albert hurried to check on the fairy dragon. Its eyes were spinning as it lay on the ground.

"Kurukururu!"

A girl emerged from the bushes.

"I'm all right...," the fairy dragon said, rising unsteadily on its four legs. It quickly hurried between Albert and the girl, as though to protect her.

"Wait. I'm an adventurer sent to look for that girl by her parents," Albert said.

"My parents sent you?!"

Albert quickly tried to explain the situation.

"But the forest is dangerous!" argued the fairy dragon, its round eyes still spinning as it scanned around.

Albert chuckled a little at the adorable gesture.

"It's okay. If you're worried about the ogres, then I took care of them."

"!!!" The fairy dragon jumped into the air and spun around. Albert was relieved that things had ended before the girl came to harm.

"I was a bit worried when I saw monster tracks. I'm glad you're safe."

Unlike seabogeys, ogres weren't especially powerful.

A D-rank party could have handled this in Albert's stead. However, ogres didn't wait to eat children the way seabogeys did. Typically, when a kid went missing in woods inhabited by ogres, they were presumed dead.

Albert looked at the fairy dragon. "You saved her, didn't you?"

A young girl who had yet to connect with her blessing had managed to survive with ogres around. It was undoubtedly because the little fairy dragon had kept her hidden.

Despite their size, fairy dragons were a type of fay, and they could cast illusions. Ogres were highly susceptible to such magic, owing to their low intelligence. That was how a relatively weak fay had managed to protect the girl.

It would have died had it come under attack, though.

Albert took inspiration from the fairy dragon's courage.

Chapter 4: Confusion and Then Rampage

"Right! Kurukururu saved me!" the girl proclaimed.

The fairy dragon frantically covered the child's mouth to silence her. "Shh! Shh!"

Albert smiled at that. "The ogres are gone, so it's okay."

"Not that!" The fairy dragon shook its head fiercely. "There is still something scary in the forest! Everyone is scared!"

"What?"

The fairy dragon's reaction clearly suggested something worse than ogres stalked this forest. Cold sweat formed on Albert's body. His adventurer instincts told him great danger approached.

"It was around here."

He heard a voice.

An intense pressure beat against Albert from behind. Hand on the grip of his sword, Albert turned slowly.

"Sir Hero..."

It was Van the Hero and the fairy Lavender.

"Albert, you saved the child."

Van wore a bright smile, yet his voice was heavy with murder. It was enough to terrify anyone.

What is this? Is this Van the Hero? I thought I was about to lock eyes with a dragon!

Albert had ridden on the *Vendidad* with Esta.

He believed Van to be an inhumane Hero, but had never been frightened by his mere presence.

It's like the first time I encountered Ms. Ruti... A force like Ruti the Hero before she took Devil's Blessing.

After getting caught up with a contract demon, Albert had caught a glimpse of Ruti the Hero.

The next day, she'd taken the airship and left Theodora and the others behind. Ares and Theodora had chased after, using Albert as a catalyst for a locator spell. Albert recalled it all so clearly, particularly that first encounter with Ruti.

Being in the presence of a being capable of effortlessly ending his life was terrifying.

If the Hero had wished to kill Albert, Albert would have perished without a chance to resist.

That his destiny was not his own to control in that moment had brought a second wave of horror.

"Albert, is the child all right?"

"…She is."

It took a moment for Albert to find his reply. Fear dulled his thoughts. He tried to keep the gears in his mind turning while desperately searching for courage somewhere in his heart.

"That's good."

"Yes, sir. All that's left is to take the child back to her village."

Then the quest will be complete. He's scarier than usual, but there isn't anything left to fight.

The threat was gone.

"I was going to take this girl to her village. What will you do, sir?"

Van looked absent-minded, yet death still radiated from him as he replied. "The source of the evil must be slain first."

"That's right. Van came to punish evil," Lavender added.

"The source?"

The unease building in Albert intensified, and sweat gathered on his brow. Somewhere in the back of his mind, he knew this was about to get ugly.

"That fairy. It was the one who led the child into the forest."

Van pointed his sword artlessly at the fairy dragon.

"I'm sorry. I'm sorry…," it apologized with its head lowered.

The girl stood in front of the fairy dragon. "Wait! It's my fault. Please don't scold Kurukururu."

It was a heartwarming scene, but Albert also understood just how perilous the situation was. This wouldn't end with a chiding. Van intended to kill the fairy dragon.

"I imagine the fairy dragon did invite the girl into the forest, but didn't mean to harm her. It only wished to play. The fairy dragon risked its life to protect the girl from dangerous ogres." Albert did his best to fill Van in, despite his fear.

Ogres couldn't lure a girl away from her home. Albert knew the fairy dragon was responsible for that part. Fay calling children out to play wasn't unheard of. Van's monastery upbringing had surely afforded him an excellent education, so he must have seen records of such events.

"There is no denying the child was in a dangerous situation. Evil must be destroyed."

Van raised his sword.

What is this?

Albert was hit by a powerful urge to run.

This was not the Van with blind faith in the Hero and unwavering strength. This boy was unsteady—insecure.

It was a fresh kind of terror. This was the unyielding horror of humanity's strongest blessing, the Hero, running rampant.

"S-Sir Hero, please calm yourself! A fairy dragon is not a wicked monster that harms humans. It's a type of fay, like Lavender!"

"Using me to beg for its life?"

Albert looked pleadingly at Lavender, but she only responded with amusement and made no effort to intervene. She had no interest in assisting her fellow fairy.

"Albert, I'll wait ten seconds, so move. You will get hit if you stay where you are."

Van's voice was flat. Albert understood there was no room to negotiate. He could hear his own teeth chattering.

And then he shouted.

"Run! I'll stop him here!"

"You can't! You'll die, mister!"

"Just go!!!"

At Albert's desperate cry, the fairy dragon turned and fled with all its strength.

Van's eyes fell upon Albert. "It doesn't make sense. You're so scared you've forgotten to draw your sword."

Albert was stunned. He truly had forgotten to prepare himself to fight. He unsheathed his weapon slowly.

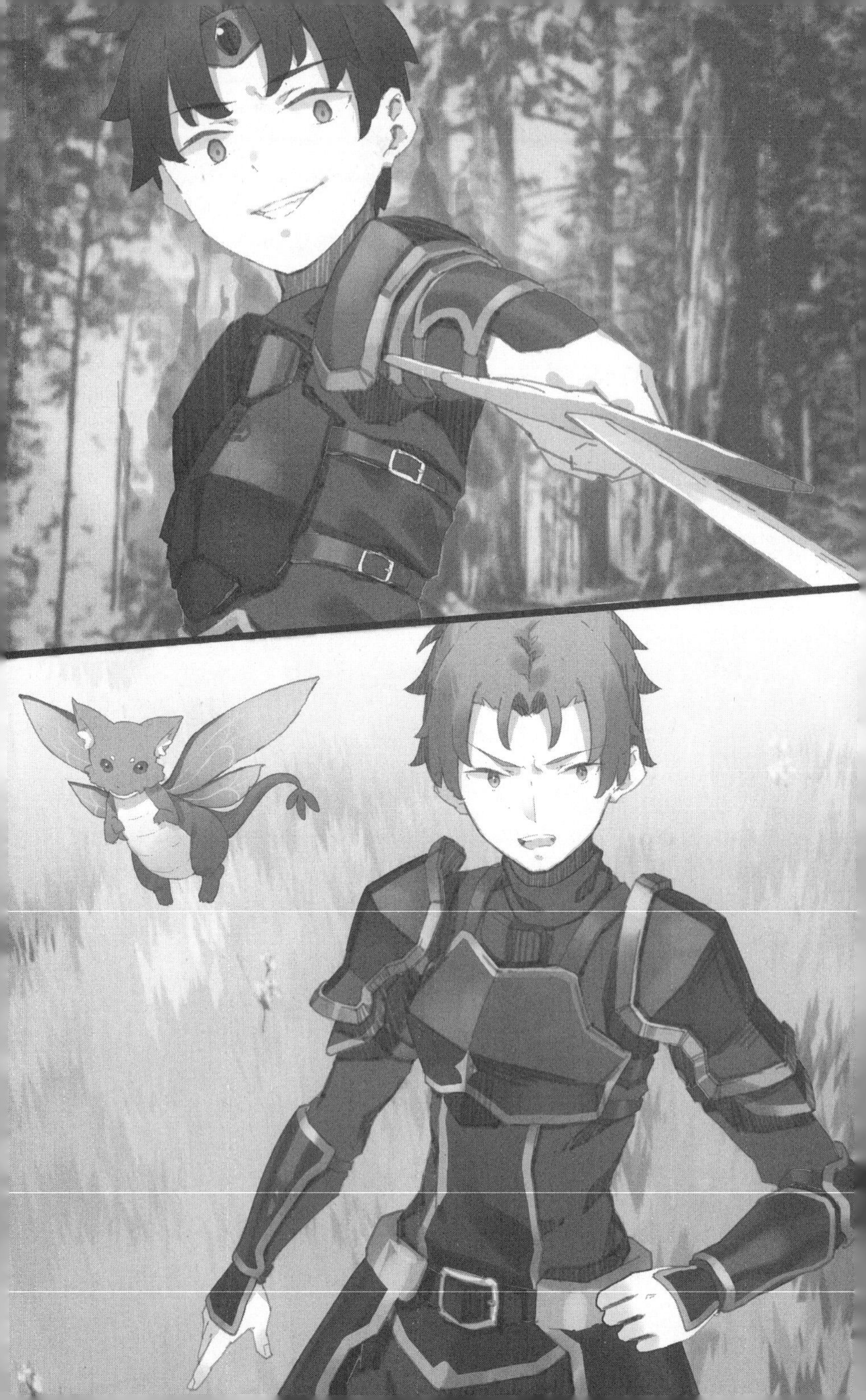

"Sir Hero, please stow your blade... That fairy only wanted to play with the child."

"Evil can't be forgiven, regardless of intent."

Albert's mind raced.

I said I would stop him, but is there anything I can actually do to stall the Hero? No, there isn't.

The culmination of everything he'd built over the course of his life likely wasn't even enough to survive a single blow. It wouldn't be enough for the fairy dragon to escape.

"Sir Hero, can you not at least wait until Cardinal Ljubo or Lady Esta arrives? It should be fine to decide after hearing your comrades' thoughts."

The only recourse was to stall by talking.

"Do you know that creature?" Van questioned, ignoring Albert's words.

Something was off. Van appeared on the cusp of some manner of significant change. Albert couldn't glean much beyond that, however. All he could do was delay the Hero with words.

"No, this is the first time I've met it."

Don't stop talking. You have to say something else.

"There were rumors of fairies in the nearby villages, but I never put much faith in them until I saw one today. You know, they supposedly hate the Wall at the End of the World."

"..."

Van showed no interest in Albert's desperate story.

"Albert, do you possess some hidden strength that you believe will allow you to defeat me?"

The two were both in one-sided conversations.

But I can't stop talking...

"I don't. I'm not a hero like you and the others."

"But your blessing is the Champion."

"I have a poor affinity with my blessing... I was unable to become a hero."

"Then why are you trying to die here?"

This is the end.

Albert exhaled hard to vent the terror of death pooling in him.

"Hah... Good question. I'm so scared I might vomit."

"Exactly. Your blessing isn't compelling you to stand in my way, and it's not because of friendship with that fairy or a lack of fear, either. You don't seem to have a death wish, so why?"

Why?

Albert had already asked himself that question, and the answer was obvious.

"Because I'm one of the Hero's comrades."

"What do you mean?"

"Even if I am no hero myself, I am still one of the Hero's allies. I cannot stand by while an innocent life is taken. If I ran, I'd be unworthy as a member of the Hero's party. I'm the only one here who can fight, so I will."

Van's expression changed for the first time.

"What is this feeling? I don't understand it." Van looked down, the hand around his sword grip trembling. "I don't understand it, but I think I want to kill you."

Van looked at Albert. He was looking not at the Champion blessing, but at Albert the person—an enemy.

"Martial Art: Holy Blade!"

The vertical slash carried a dreadful power, but it was a straightforward attack.

"Martial Art: Block Tackle!"

Albert's response was a defense technique that matched an opponent's attack, then knocked them back.

His sword was plain, but it was a quality piece that Esta had picked out. It could withstand a blow from a giant, yet the Hero's skill shattered it.

"Gh!"

Albert felt a searing pain in his side.

His response saved him from immediate death, but Van's sword still reached his internal organs.

I'll die from blood loss without magic, but I'm still alive for the moment.

"Raaaaaaaaargh!!!!!!!" Albert roared as he rammed into Van.

They both knew that Albert's strength wasn't enough to move the Hero.

Thus, Van made no effort to dodge.

"What?!" Van exclaimed. He hadn't expected Albert's follow-up.

Albert clung to the Hero's body. He wasn't grappling with the boy in an attempt to sweep his legs or trying to pin his joints. Albert simply wrapped his arms around Van's back and held on as firmly as he could.

"What are you doing?!"

"You can't chase the fairy dragon with me on you!"

"!"

Van tried to break free.

"Urgggggghhhh!!!!"

"Get off!"

For all Van's might, he couldn't tear Albert away.

Albert gripped with more than his hands. He bit into the edge of Van's armor, blood dripping from his mouth as he fought against the Hero's power with his whole body.

"Why would you go so far?"

Van already knew the answer: because Albert was one of the Hero's comrades.

He raised his sword.

"Urghhhhh!!!"

A muffled scream rose out of Albert's throat. Van's holy sword had pierced his back.

"Let go."

Albert refused.

"Let go, let go."

Van stabbed him over, and over, and over again.

Albert's consciousness dimmed under the weight of the searing pain and icy death.

Yet his hands would not yield. This was the only way he could stop the Hero.

As long as I don't let go...I can still fight.

Albert was the Hero's comrade. That was why he could fight.

"I'm the Hero! Why are you doing this?! For the sake of a single fairy?!"

Albert wished he could answer, but he lacked the energy to speak.

You aren't the Hero I'm talking about. I mean the Hero that Lady Esta searches for, the one she's trying to guide. The Hero who has yet to appear... If she intends to be that Hero's ally, then I have to be a man worthy of being an ally, too, if I'm going to stay with her.

Albert couldn't convey that feeling as he endured the pain, but he could persist. He fought back death, hoping to stall for even a moment longer.

"Dammit!"

For the first time in his life, Van cursed.

For a boy who accepted every outrage and tribulation as the will of God, it was as good as admitting defeat. And that disturbed his already troubled heart further.

"Van!" Lavender shouted, but Van saw nothing other than Albert.

"Agh..."

Esta's spear pierced the Hero's neck.

"You fought well," Esta whispered as she held Albert's body.

The strength faded from Albert's arms, and Esta carried him away. She gently lay him on the ground, and, gathering as much magic power as she could, she formed a spell.

"Regenerate."

The advanced magic possessed an effect similar to Healing Hands. Mortal wounds beyond the power of ordinary spells began to close.

"Albert, I am truly glad to have met you."

Esta conjured another spell to summon a spirit drake.

"Grrrr."

The creature used its fangs dexterously to place both Albert, and then the young girl who was standing there petrified, onto its back.

"Young miss," Esta said to the crying child. The poor girl had been paralyzed with terror while witnessing Albert's vain struggle, too frightened to even run.

"Could you please look after him? He's a very special person to me."

"Okay…"

The girl nodded while tears ran down her cheeks. She understood that this adult woman, who was likely very strong, was counting on her. The girl couldn't help but cry, but she knew she had to respond to this woman.

"Thank you, I appreciate it."

The spirit drake took flight.

While that was happening, Van healed his injury with Healing Hands and stood back up.

"Esta."

Van looked stunned.

"The fairy dragon lured that child out into the forest, so I decided it needed to die."

"Van."

Esta leveled her spear at him.

"Gh!!"

Clang!

Weapons met and sparks flew.

"Esta…"

"Did you think I wouldn't be angry?"

Esta's attack had been meant to kill, and Van was shocked to realize as much.

"I'm livid." Esta employed the many spear techniques she'd honed against Van, not holding anything back.

"Esta!"

She'd always been sincere about helping Van become the Hero, and while they often disagreed, he respected her for that.

And now Esta was an enemy. Van suddenly realized that he'd never heeded her advice. For the first time, something heavy weighed on his heart.

"Unease? Me? Even though my blessing is the Hero?"

Van wondered if he'd made a mistake somewhere along the way. The thought wormed its way deep into his mind. The Hero, who should've been incapable of faltering, was doubting himself.

"Van! What's wrong?!" Lavender cried.

The boy's sword was passive and unmotivated, a far cry from his usual fighting style. The Van who relied on Healing Hands and fought unafraid of being wounded was nowhere to be seen as he shrank back.

"It seems you aren't in your usual form, but I won't go easy on you."

Esta understood killing Van would cause a huge problem, yet she couldn't stop herself. She'd never felt like this before. Feelings raged within her, unbound and uncontrollable, yet her spear had never moved with such deadly precision.

It jabbed calmly and cleanly with the simple intent to kill.

Esta was overpowering the Hero.

I intended to be the Hero's ally, but it seems I'm fated to be the Hero's enemy.

Esta's spear shot forward, tearing across Van's body.

"Ngh!"

He stumbled backward as blood flew.

"This is it."

Esta's weapon took aim at the Hero's heart.

"Get away from Van!!!" Lavender screamed, and lightning bolts came crashing down toward Esta.

"Oh?"

Esta stuck her spear into the ground and cast a defensive spell. A moment later, the lightning dissipated, and Esta stood without a scratch.

"Using the spear as a lightning rod?! Pretty tricky for someone who's lost it!!!"

"What about you? I thought you didn't want to get serious in front of Van?"

Chapter 4: Confusion and Then Rampage

"Shut up! I always hated you!"

"A magic duel, huh? Fine."

Esta was maintaining the spirit drake, so summoning magic was off-limits for the time being. Spells were influenced by a user's mental state. And Esta was confident that, at present, she could wield attack magic that would rival Ares's.

"Wither and crumble! Haboob!"

"Holy light, thy name is death, become a blade that reaps mine enemy! Death!"

Lavender unleashed sandstorm magic that tore at the flesh while Esta completed powerful death magic.

Red sand and white death clashed, spreading destruction all around them.

Both were feats of magic that Lavender and Esta wouldn't ordinarily use.

While maintaining her magic, Esta also readied her spear in her right hand. Meanwhile, Lavender gathered spirits around her so that she might use her true strength. This was something different from magic.

"What...do I want? Hero within me, please tell me." Seeing two allies locked in battle, Van could only question himself.

Defeat Esta? Protect Lavender? Stop the battle? Kill them both?

Communicating via impulse, the Hero blessing in Van told him to "Just fight."

Fight? Why? For whom?

No one here needed the Hero. But the Hero had to fight. Fight and grow their blessing. Fight even greater evil. And die.

As he watched Lavender and Esta battle, Van figured it out.

"I understand."

Van stood and held his sword.

"I understand. I...am angry."

Van didn't comprehend why, but he'd been angry since that day with the seabogeys. And now that he was aware of the feeling, all that remained was to act upon it.

"Hrahhhhh!!!!!!!!!!!!!" He roared, leaping at Esta.

"Come, then!!!" Esta parried his sword with her spear.

"Lavender! With me!"

"Van?! Understood!"

Van had cooperated with his party members before. However, this was the first time he had truly fought in sync with a comrade. He aimed strikes at Esta after Lavender's magic created openings, and he guarded the fairy so she had time to cast. Van displayed tremendous growth in this battle.

"So this is the Hero. But it matters not!!!" Esta didn't cede so much as a single step, withstanding Van and Lavender's teamwork. "No slipshod combination will work on me!!!"

The battle raged, with neither side relinquishing anything.

Trees were mowed down, and the creatures of the forest fled. The land cried out as the greatest powers on the continent clashed.

And before long...

"That's enough."

A wall of water erupted between the two sides.

There was a thundering crash, and Esta, Van, and Lavender were forced to fall back to avoid being caught in the flood.

"Undine!" Lavender glared up in the air.

A woman with a translucent figure hovered there. Undine, archfay of water, peered down at the three.

"Cooled your head?"

Van and Lavender watched Undine with narrowed eyes.

Esta, however, exhaled and lowered her spear. "Yes, I've calmed down."

"Esta!"

Van shouted at her for daring to quit the fight. He wanted to keep going.

"No, the battle is over... Look."

Esta's shoulders relaxed.

The surrounding forest was in ruins.

"As the representative of all who live in this land, I will not allow you to battle here anymore," Undine declared.

"Hah! A mere water archfay thinks she can get in my way?!" Lavender flew up into the air to stare down Undine. "Don't act all high and mighty just because you're some primordial being!"

"And I suppose it is only natural a manifestation of destruction such as yourself would think herself superior. I admit, seeing you in a more adorable form is quite pleasant, though."

"Youuuu!"

"Oh dear, what a waste of such a pretty face. Are you that scared of your beloved Van discovering your true identity?"

"I'll kill you!"

Lavender began to work a spell.

"Huh?"

A javelin pierced her body before her work was complete, however.

"Ghhk! Ghah...!"

"Lavender!"

Van caught the fairy as she fell.

"This isn't..."

"Yes, that body's death isn't enough to kill you. But if it goes, so does your adorable figure."

"...!"

Lavender's eyes were bloodshot, and she attempted another spell.

"Gah?!"

A second javelin penetrated the barrier of wind Lavender had created around herself and Van, piercing Lavender's body and Van's hand.

"Could it be...her?"

Van felt it.

This was the work of the girl who'd defeated him. The one he'd had a divine revelation about. The one he was duty bound to kill as the Hero.

Van couldn't sense her. Undoubtedly, she was skilled at concealing her presence. He was certain she was somewhere in the direction the javelin had come from, though. She had to be that way, just out of sight.

I want to fight!!!!!!

"Van...!"

Lavender wheezed painfully in the boy's hand, covered in her blood and his. Van peered at her, felt the warmth of her body, and then slowly opened his mouth.

"Understood. We'll withdraw."

Van sheathed his sword.

Chapter 5

The Hero's Challenge

It was evening in the fairy village, and Albert was resting peacefully on a bed.

"His body is recovering well. Your magic reached to the depths of his wounds," I said to Esta after completing a thorough examination.

"Then why isn't he opening his eyes?"

"It's just a matter of energy. He fought hard and fiercely against Van. I'm guessing he gave every bit of strength he could to keep going. He needs time to rest."

"I see... Thank goodness." Esta breathed a sigh of relief.

"You did well to notice, Ruti."

"Mhm."

Van's movement had been sudden. He and Lavender had headed off without any sign or provocation. Yarandrala, who'd been watching them, didn't get an indication they were headed for Ruti or us. All she could do was inform Esta of this development. She never noticed that something was off about Van.

Esta pursued Van after that, and they wound up fighting.

Fortunately, Ruti had noticed something odd about Van's behavior and followed him, too. In the process, she ran into Undine, who was protecting the fairy dragon Kurukururu, and helped her from the shadows, forcing Van and Lavender to retreat.

Once the immediate threat was gone, Undine and Ruti took Albert to the fairy village for protection while Esta returned to Zoltan to inform us of what had happened. Once everyone was caught up, we all headed to the fairy village.

Ruti, Esta, and I were in the room with Albert, but everyone else was on guard, watching the village.

"It was just intuition," Ruti added. Perhaps she'd subconsciously recognized something amiss in Van because of her Hero blessing and called it intuition.

"Well, you were right."

"Yes. If not for you, I don't know what I would've done," Undine said with a smile.

"I had to stay hidden and couldn't use any magic unique to the Hero, so it helped that you were there, too, Undine," Ruti replied.

"Hee-hee. Let's call it good teamwork, then."

Undine cheerfully held Ruti's hand and patted it. Ruti looked mildly annoyed.

"Umm..."

"Hmm?"

There was a voice. A small dragon poked its head into the room.

"Kurukururu."

"Is Mr. Adventurer okay?"

"The woman in the mask here healed him, so he'll be fine. He's just tired," I answered brightly to put Kurukururu at ease.

"Come in, Kurukururu. Go see your hero."

At Undine's beckoning, Kurukururu's butterfly wings fluttered, and the fairy dragon landed on Albert's pillow.

"Thank you, Mr. Adventurer. Thank you."

Kurukururu put its head on Albert's cheek and offered words of gratitude over and over.

There was no denying that Albert had saved the creature's life.

"I always knew Albert was a hero."

Back when he was Zoltan's B-rank adventurer, I believed he had the potential to be a hero. To witness it bloom at last was a happy moment.

"That's right, Albert is a hero… While I…"
"Esta?"
She left the room.
Maybe I should talk with her…

*   *   *

"Esta."
She was peering out the door's window in the next room. Beyond the pane formed of water, fairies flitted around Rit, playing with her. Looking closely, I spied Mister Crawly Wawly riding one of the fairy dragons. He held a small twig like a lance and wore a walnut shell for a helmet with a sharp look on his face…just like a fairy knight of legend.

"Heh. What an interesting spider. I never really paid much attention to him before," Esta remarked with a smile. "I see things far more clearly now than I used to."

"That's a good thing, isn't it?"

"I think so. But today is the first time I ever lost myself in rage." Esta's expression turned pained. "I had considered the possibility that Albert might end up fighting Van. All I ever intended was to heal Albert, beat Van back, and then retreat. That's all. But…Albert was far more grievously wounded than I could have imagined… When I saw him on the verge of death like that, I…"

"You couldn't stop yourself?"

"I was terrified."

Esta changed positions so no one outside would see her, then removed her mask. There were tears in her eyes.

"I was terrified of losing Albert. Even now, the thought of it is heartrending. I tried to kill you to force Ruti to continue being the Hero…but this is more frightening than anything else."

"You're scared?"

"Yes. Scared that I will make another mistake eventually. And that the next one might be impossible to fix…"

"Then do you think you can forget your feelings for Albert?"

Esta's shoulders trembled. "...What would you do?"

"In my case, the question would be if I could forget about Rit... Well, the answer's easy enough." I smiled. "There's no way I could forget. These feelings are more precious than anything. I might worry how to deal with the emotions on occasion, but I can't forget them."

"Yeah...I suppose not." Esta's expression softened, and she broke into a smile. "I don't think I'll be able to forget, either."

"That's a good thing, isn't it? That emotion comes from the heart. It's entirely separate from things like Divine Blessings."

"A feeling separate from blessings... Heh. I've become a pretty terrible cleric. Perhaps it's because I met all of you."

"Even Cardinal Ljubo enjoys the company of women."

"Don't lump me in with him!"

We both laughed.

A thought occurred to me. "Speaking of..."

"What?"

"We both found our first loves pretty late."

"Sheesh... And here I was wondering what you'd say."

"What? What? Something fun?"

We laughed again, and the fairies outside gathered at the window, curious about what was happening.

Mister Crawly Wawly, still riding the fairy dragon, leaped into the air happily when he saw Esta grinning.

※ ※ ※

Ljubo angrily paced around his rented room in a tavern in the heart of Zoltan.

"What's going on? What happened to my Hero?"

When he heard that Van had attacked Albert and gotten into a fight with Esta, Ljubo was at a loss.

He'd planned to wait for the Hero to grow, to raise Van before engaging the demon lord's army with the church's forces, to arrange things optimally.

Ljubo's goal lay beyond the demon lord's defeat. He would become the most powerful man in the church, the highest ruler on the continent, and claim the seat of the church father.

The cardinals selected the father. Ljubo's backing was weak, so he presently had no hope of winning. That would change if he was a comrade to the Hero who slew the demon lord.

Once Van succeeded, no one would bar him from becoming God's proxy.

Where did I go wrong?

"I can still fix this."

Even if he had to abandon Esta, this could still work out, so long as he had the Hero.

"Right, what about adding Danan and Gideon to the party? They're both trash that can't keep up with the Hero, but they should be sufficient as temporary members to tide us over."

Ljubo felt that solution was satisfying. And no sooner had he decided as much than there was a knock on his door.

"Cardinal Ljubo."

"Van? What is it?"

"There is something I would like to report."

"Report?"

Ljubo was worried about what else might have happened as he opened the door. Outside the door were Van and Lavender, packed up and ready to leave.

"Van, what is…?"

"I've decided to leave Zoltan."

"O-ohh! You've finally come around?!" Ljubo nodded with a broad smile. "That is a wise decision. I can find you countless other enemies to raise your blessing level. Losing Esta is unfortunate, but I have a lead on some replacements. Just leave that to me."

Ljubo was in high spirits, but Van didn't react to what he was saying at all.

"We're going to Undine's lair."

"What?"

"I will kill all of the fay there. Esta, Gideon, and the rest of them are there, so I will kill all of them, too."

"Van… What are you saying?"

"If I do that, the ancient elf creation will surely appear, and I will kill it. If it doesn't come, then I will destroy Zoltan until it does. Once it's dead, I'll leave Zoltan."

"Calm down, Van! You're the Hero!"

Ljubo desperately tried to explain the proper path for the Hero. And Van replied this time, in a way.

"Agh…"

Heat bloomed in Ljubo's stomach. Looking down, he saw his clothes turning red.

"Argh, Van… Why…?"

His body shuddered, and he fell to the floor with a heavy thud.

Van held the replica holy sword Ljubo had gifted him. Blood dripped from its blade onto the floor.

"I don't feel the impulses of the Hero anymore. My blessing no longer tells me what I should do."

With the last of his strength, Ljubo looked up at Van. The boy's expression was hollow. Ljubo understood things had progressed far beyond the point where he could course-correct.

"So I will do the last thing the Hero asked of me… I will kill that girl…and all the evil in my way."

Ljubo could no longer answer.

Van observed the growing puddle of blood. Lavender leaned gently against his cheek.

"Van…I will always be on your side."

If Van continued like this, he would be destroyed. But Lavender was resolved to support him. Because she believed that was what love meant.

* * *

An hour later, at the fairy village.

Everyone gathered to discuss our next move while Albert rested.

"Van is coming."

The others nodded when I said that.

"Undine has put up her barrier, but Van and Lavender will break through."

"Indeed. Lavender is a greater fay than I."

"Greater than the archfay of water…"

Undine ruled over one of the four great elements that made up the world. Someone with a higher blessing level might be stronger than she, but to be a greater fay… I could only think of a handful of possibilities.

Rit raised her hand. "Undine?"

"Yes?"

"What exactly is Lavender?"

Undine seemed a little bit troubled by the question. "I thought it best not to reveal that child's identity if she kept it quiet, but I suppose the time for that courtesy is long behind us… Yes, I will answer you."

Rit and I leaned forward in anticipation.

"Her true nature is calamity."

"Calamity?"

"Lavender's real name is Ketu, the archfay of calamity. Most of our kind are part of nature and possess a demeanor that fosters life. However, Ketu is a being that knows only pure destruction and power."

Ketu, the archfay of calamity. I'd never heard of such a creature.

"Archfay of destruction have rampaged across this world since its birth. However, they were wiped out by dragons and ancient elves. She is the only one left. By the time of the wood elves, she had retreated to the depths of a jungle and hidden her power from others."

"So that's why there are no records of her in the kingdom's library," I said.

She was a being from myth. The legendary Hero and a fabled fairy.

"Really? She's actually that big a deal?"

Danan was getting more excited while I was growing worried.

"…Let's focus on the immediate issue," Tisse said, turning to me. "Van and Lavender are coming to attack. What will we do?"

"This is my third time negotiating with Van. It's time to settle things."

"Negotiating? He is coming to kill Undine! I do not think there's much room for talk!"

"That's true. This will definitely turn into a fight…"

I looked at Danan and Esta. I still remembered the first time I'd met them.

"I fought both of you once, before you joined the party."

The two of them looked surprised but quickly smiled as they recalled those old battles.

"And Rit, you fought Ruti in the colosseum."

"I suppose I did. I was completely overwhelmed, though…"

My bout with Danan had taken place during a martial arts tournament.

To locate a demon that was hiding in a town, I'd joined a tournament while Ruti and the others searched other places nearby, including the local lord's castle. I'd fought Danan in the championship, and afterward, we battled the demon together. That was the impetus for him to join the party.

The fight with Esta had been at the Last Wall fortress. The demon lord's armies, wary of Ruti, had manipulated a cardinal into declaring her a heretic posing as the Hero and sentencing her to execution. Esta, who was a holy knight of the church and spear-fighting instructor, stood against us as the weapon of the church. However, through that battle, she came to understand Ruti truly was the Hero. She disobeyed the church's orders and worked with us.

"Compared with Danan and Esta, my picking a fight with Ruti to damage her reputation sounds kind of petty," Rit admitted.

"It doesn't just sound petty. It really was."

"Guh." Rit slumped at Ruti's merciless remark. "Ugh, so harsh."

"It's payback for everything you said back then."

"When you put it like that, I suppose I have no right to complain."

Rit and Ruti grinned.

Despite fighting in the past, the two could now talk and smile together without reservation.

"You aren't seriously going to suggest we can reach an understanding with Van by fighting him, are you?" There was a hint of reproach in Tisse's voice. "That's a bit optimistic."

"True, if it was the old Van, then nothing would change by our battling him. But there's a chance of getting through to him now."

"A chance? It sounds like he's on a rampage."

"That's right. He's running wild. The Hero who should not waver or doubt himself has lost control."

Van's faith in the righteousness of Divine Blessings had caused all sorts of problems, but to attack Albert, his own comrade, to get at a weak fairy that hadn't harmed anyone, went beyond the Hero's role.

Van was acting outside the boundaries God had set for the Hero.

"He's lost. My words have a chance of reaching him. It's possible we can change his extreme views."

"But…," Tisse objected.

"I trust Red."

"If it goes wrong, I'll step in. Please, leave this to Big Brother."

Tisse let out a little laugh at Rit and Ruti's remarks. "Then I guess I have no choice but to trust him, too… All right. How do you intend to fight him?"

"About that… I have a favor to ask of all of you."

"Hey, you only need to ask!" Danan said.

"I'm going to settle things with Van in a duel. If Lavender tries to interfere, I want you to stop her."

"A duel? That's crazy, even for you."

"Van is strong, and there are no absolutes in combat, so I won't say I'll definitely win, but…I'm going to win."

"Whenever you talk like this, things always work out." Rit squeezed my hand. "Leave Lavender to us. We'll stop her no matter what."

"Thanks. I'm counting on you all."

Okay, it's time for the final battle!

          *   *   *

Dark, heavy clouds filled the sky.

"Scatter."

Lavender wore a nasty smirk on her face.

Countless lightning bolts, tornadoes, and sandstorms pummeled the area around the lake where Undine lived.

The torrent of energy was so powerful that even Undine's barrier guarding the lake shattered in an instant. Cracks spread along Lavender's body as it strained against the enormity of her gathered magic power. It didn't appear to hurt her at all, however. It was as though the chains fettering her true nature were coming free.

The storm settled, and the dust cleared.

"Hmph... The one from before is here."

The lake was entirely unscathed, as though nothing had happened. Ruti's Sacred Shield had warded off Lavender's destruction magic. Rit, Tisse, Danan, Yarandrala, Esta, Ruti, and I stood before the village, all watching Van.

"I finally found you." Van beamed when he laid eyes on Ruti. "It was quite the roundabout path, and I have become confused...but I am sure that if I kill you, I will be able to return to being the Hero."

"..."

Ruti answered Van with a cold gaze. She had no interest in speaking to him.

"I am the Hero... Do you have nothing to say to me?" Van wanted her to reply. The old Van wouldn't have cared.

"Van." I spoke instead of Ruti.

"Gideon, I finally understand."

"..."

"She is Ruti the Hero!" Van shouted.

Van had reached Ruti the Hero at last.

"This is the fate that Almighty Demis has set before me! To become the true Hero, I must defeat the one who has grown old! Van the Hero will inherit the strength that Ruti the Hero has gathered and then save the world!"

Van was growing agitated, but his outburst struck me as hollow.

I walked toward him. "Van, come clean."

"Gideon, what are you talking about?"

"You don't know what to do. Not as the Hero, not as a devout believer, and not as the human named Van. You're lost and compensating by making up an excuse to explain what you're feeling."

"That's not true at all!"

"It is! If I'm wrong, then tell me what the Hero inside you wants!"

"It's telling me to defeat Ruti!"

"Wrong! You don't feel any such impulse!"

Van raised his sword and leveled a tremendous murderous intent at me.

"As the Guide, allow me to lead you through your doubt."

My expression remained firm, despite Van's rising power.

"You made me this way. It's all because I talked with you."

"I know."

"It hurts to be unsure. It's like I'm losing myself."

"I know."

"So…I won't speak with you anymore. I'm going to kill you to make this pain go away."

"Van, you've grown up in a small world. A world of faith with no room for doubt. However, it's natural for people to question things during their lives… If you are the Hero, then don't flee from the pain of doubt."

"…!"

"Did you think we never wavered during our fight against the demon lord's army? We doubted ourselves every step of the way. 'Is this really enough?' 'Can we really trust our judgment?' We felt the creeping tendrils of apprehension time and again. And regret ate at our hearts, too. Still, the Hero must not run from their doubt."

"But Ruti the Hero never faltered!"

"Ruti wasn't sure, and she struggled. Yet she stood firm anyway, and so the stories claimed that Ruti the Hero never wavered."

"I don't believe you! The Hero doesn't falter! That's the role God set for us!"

"You're wrong. The people who fought alongside Ruti didn't take heart because of her Hero blessing. It's because she stood firm against her doubts!"

"She endured?"

"No matter how painful it got, she never fled. She pushed forward with the strength of her will alone. That's what people call courage."

Van's face twisted with rage.

"Courage? The Hero has Immunity to Fear… Isn't that enough?!"

I removed my cloak and grabbed the second bronze sword I wore beneath it. I tossed the weapon to Van.

"What are you doing?"

"Van, I challenge you to a duel. Take the blade."

"This is a cheap bronze sword."

"This battle is between the Hero and the Guide, a battle of blessings. Let's fight on equal terms. If we do, I'm sure it will resolve your doubt."

"…If the Hero wins, it means I no longer require the Guide."

I held up both hands, showing that I had no magic equipment.

"I understand." Van cast aside his holy sword. Then he removed his armor and removed his enchanted rings and amulets.

"Now it's fair."

Van picked up the bronze sword I had given him and assumed a stance.

"All right." I drew my own bronze sword and stood ready.

"Van! Don't let him trick you!" Lavender shouted as she flew around.

"Stay back, Lavender."

"Rit!"

The fairy found herself faced with the sharp end of a shotel.

"Don't get in my way! I'll kill you!"

"Don't interfere with their fight. The two of them agreed to settle this with a duel. We don't have any right to stop them."

"Shut up! Shut up! Everyone who gets in the way of my love should just die!"

Lavender's eyes shot wide, and cracks spread from them across her entire face.

Even at a distance, I could tell the giant being restrained within was breaking free.

However, Rit didn't budge.

"I won't allow anyone to get in the way of my love. Whether it's a legendary fay, the demon lord, or God himself. If they threaten our love, I'll face them just like I am you."

Rit had always been the sort of princess who'd sneak away from the castle to be an adventurer. And seeing her gallant figure at that moment, I fell in love with her all over again.

Rit and the others trust me. I should focus on Van.

"Let's finish this, Van."

"Don't expect me to show mercy if you stop at the last moment and admit defeat."

"I don't. This is a real duel, one that will only end when you or I can't move any longer. If you stop at the last second, I'll use that opening to cut you down."

"Good!" Van moved first. "I won't stop until I release this anger!"

He disappeared.

A martial art!

"Swallow's Approach!"

Van closed the distance between us in an instant and brought his sword down. His bronze blade clanged as I deflected the blow.

A glow enveloped his weapon while our swords pushed against each other.

Trying to break my sword by empowering his.

"Hahhhh!"

"You've stepped in too far!"

I beat Van's sword to the left. His blade was impatient. Van's desire to cut me down was too strong. There was no mind controlling his weapon.

"Kh!"

My sword bit into Van's shoulder.

There was a spurt of red blood, and he grimaced for a moment.

Ordinarily, he would've been protected by armor, but this was a battle without such equipment. The best chance to strike changed depending on the situation, and Van couldn't deal with that.

"You're weak when it comes to defense."

I aimed attacks for spots usually protected.

Van's fighting style already disregarded defense, and he knew nothing of protecting himself without armor.

His attacks relied on the Divine Blessing God had granted him. There was no human-developed method behind his form.

"Gahhhh!!!"

His body was stained red from spilled blood. My sword had cut into his skin dozens of times, yet he remained standing. The Hero wouldn't lose heart so quickly.

"Judgment Lightning!"

Magic, at this range?!

"Ughhh!!!!"

The lightning scorched my body, but I held on to keep from passing out and thrust my sword.

"Argh!"

It landed!

My blade pierced Van's right shoulder while he was occupied casting the spell. The bronze sword tore through muscles and reached bone.

"Uwahhhhh!"

Van's face twisted. His right arm would be useless now.

I'd like to follow that up, but...

"Hahhhh, hahhh..."

That spell had taken its toll on me. My feet were heavy, and I fell to one knee. I somehow managed to slash upward from that crouch, but Van had already moved out of range.

"You aren't getting away!"

In this state, it'll be bad if I let him get away to fire off more magic!

I poured strength into my unsteady legs and chased him down with Lightning Speed.

He should be reaching his limit. The next blow will decide it.

"Stoppppppp!!!" Lavender screamed. The black fog erupting from her body was forming into a giant figure.

"Get away from Vaaaaan!"

The dark mist grasped for me, but I was completely focused on Van.

"I won't let you!"

"No you don't."

Rit and Ruti cut into Lavender's arm.

They would stop her.

"Hrahhhh!!!" I roared as my sword came down.

"…Martial Art." Van's eyes opened, and he looked at me. The bronze sword in his left hand released an odd sound.

Not good!

"Great Whirlwind!!!!!!"

We're going to hit each other at the same time!

If I continued my strike, I'd deal Van a mortal blow, but his skill would rip through my torso.

He's willing to sacrifice himself for a sure kill… Gh!

"Gahhhhh!!!"

I pulled back my sword and defended against Van's slash.

My sword shattered, and blood erupted from my body.

"Red!!!" Rit screamed from somewhere I couldn't see.

The broken blade fell to the ground with a clatter.

"I win!!!" Van shouted.

Blood poured from my chest, and my body was quickly losing strength.

Lavender laughed triumphantly. "What now, Rit?! If you don't go help, your lover will die!"

"Red." I could tell that Rit was looking at me. "You can do it! Don't lose, Red!"

Heat and strength returned to my body.

Van had dropped his bronze sword to lay his left hand on my arm.

"This is the end! Healing Hands Mastery: Reversal!"

This was Van's trump card, a skill that pushed all his damage onto someone else. It was the embodiment of Van's ideal Hero, one who could overcome any situation.

Van's body glowed with the power of the Hero's blessing.

"I win!"

However...

"I was waiting for that."

My body glowed with the light of Healing Hands, too, while the light of Van's ability disappeared.

"Skill nullification?!"

Skill nullification was a technique whereby two instances of the same skill clashed and nullified each other. There weren't many opportunities to use it in practice, though.

For the phenomenon to work, the skills had to come from the same blessing. In other words, a Mage's Fireball and a Sage's Fireball could not nullify each other.

This trick offset a blessing's activation before it manifested physically.

"I had Ruti imbue me with the power of Healing Hands beforehand."

That meant I could only pull this off once, but that was all I needed. Van, so sure of his victory, had dropped his sword. He'd never even thought to protect himself.

"It's my win!!!"

I plunged my broken bronze sword down at him. It ripped deep into his body before he could react.

"Kuh... Hah..."

It was a heavy wound. Blood poured from it, and Van collapsed.

"Wasn't this supposed to be a match between the Hero and the Guide alone...?" the boy asked.

"Obviously, that was a trick. We both wielded bronze swords, but I have more experience using one, and I'm more accustomed to fighting without armor. This was never an even battle. This was all so I could defeat you."

"Dammit... That's dirty..."

"Van, you seem to be operating under a fundamental misunderstanding. You lost because you were preoccupied with thoughts like 'because I'm the Hero' and 'because he's the Guide.'"

"I don't understand..."

"This was a battle between two people: between Van and Red. Our Divine Blessings are just one part of us. You wound up like this because you didn't understand that and only paid attention to the blessings."

"...Dammit, dammit, dammit."

"Van, has the doubt cleared?"

"Huh?"

"That emotion right there is what led you astray."

"What, this anger?"

"The anger is just a symptom. It's not the cause. I'm talking about the reason you feel angry."

"I..."

"You're frustrated, right?"

"...!"

Van stopped moving.

His eyes widened in shock. I could see the energy he'd gathered to fight wither now that he finally had his answer.

"The impetus was the connection between the roles of the Guide and the Hero, but when we were fighting seabogeys at the beach, you felt like you lost to me. You realized you would've failed to save that single child by yourself. When she offered her gratitude, you felt undeserving... That's when the frustration formed in your heart."

Van had never experienced frustration before.

Intense, fiery emotions were foreign to him because he'd spent his entire life in the secluded world of faith. He couldn't come to terms with something he didn't understand. So that frustration simmered in his heart, becoming a pain that refused to leave...until it finally exploded.

"Frus...tration...?"

"Reflect on it in your dreams... Let's talk again when you wake up."

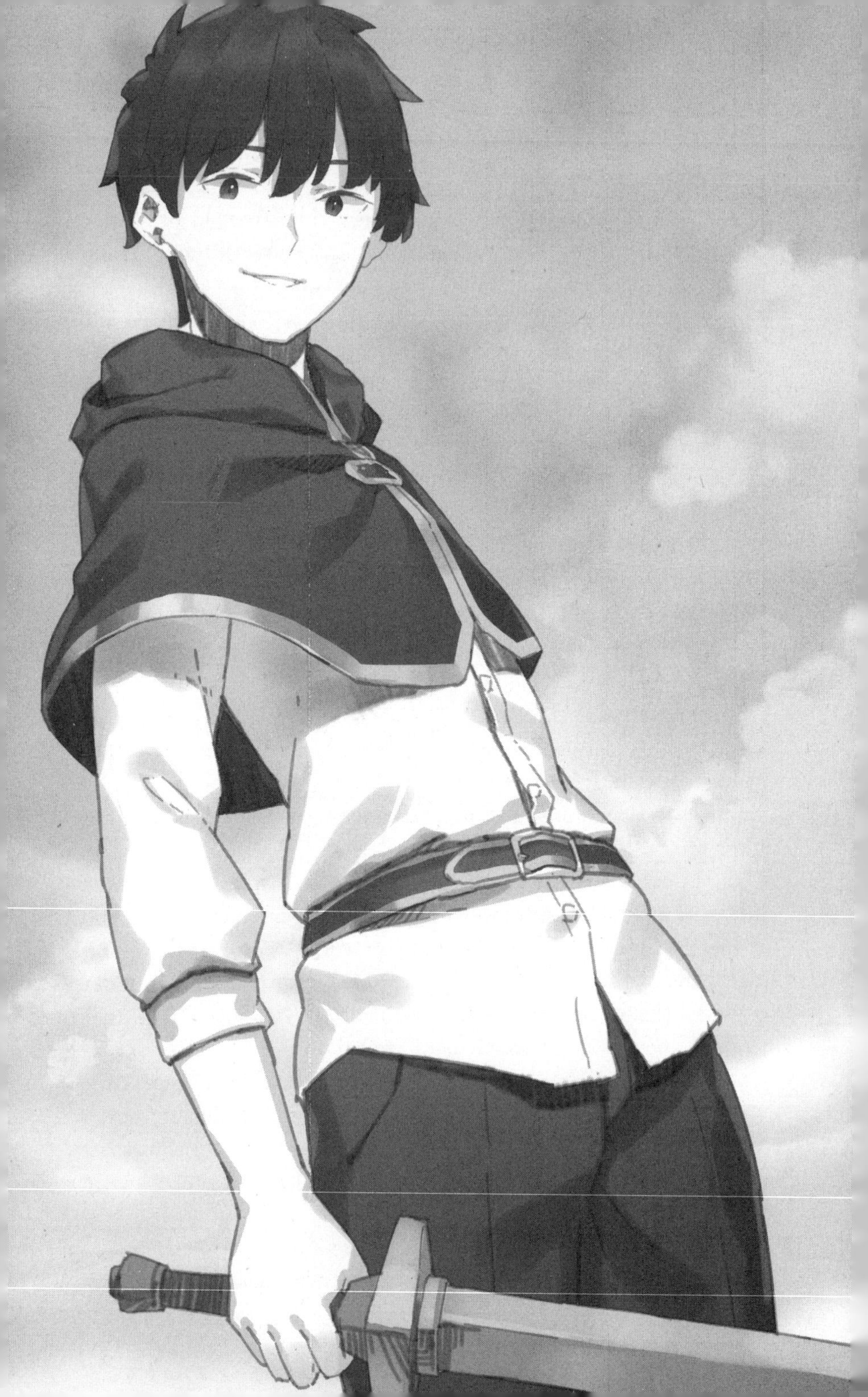

Van's body slumped.

Has he finally passed out?

"Hahhhhh…"

I let out a deep sigh and sat on the ground.

"Argh, this hurts. I'm gonna die… Fighting the Hero is exhausting."

My wound stung.

Van's self-sacrificing attack had been dangerous. Had he used anything other than a bronze sword, I would've died.

The Hero really is strong. Even with everything lined up in my favor, it still came down to the wire.

"Big Brother!"

"Red!"

I sensed Ruti and Rit rushing over to me.

We'd already discussed what to do next, so I could leave it to them.

"Van, knights can be pretty nasty." I smiled at him. "This battle is actually a draw. It just took longer for me to collapse, is all."

I'd planned out all sorts of tricks, but the biggest of all was aligning things to make a draw seem like a win.

I really don't ever want to have a fight like this again.

My consciousness faded from the blood loss.

Epilogue
Conclusion, and the Next Journey

"This is…"

A curved ceiling greeted him when he opened his eyes.

"…?!"

The first thing he noticed was that he was tied to the bed. His fingers were also bound, ensuring he couldn't move them to cast magic.

"Van!"

A small figure was clinging to his cheek.

"Lavender…"

The fairy's arms were tied with cord.

She couldn't hug him as she usually did, and so instead rubbed her little cheek against his joyously. Van had never thought this before, but he found the warmth of Lavender's gesture comforting.

"Oh, you're awake?"

Raising his head, Van saw Albert standing over him with a wooden tray.

"Water and a painkiller."

A cup and powdered medicine were on the tray, which Albert set at the bedside.

"Don't be stingy! Just let him use Healing Hands! What will you do if this leaves a scar?"

"It'd be a much bigger problem if he recovered completely and went on a rampage again."

Casting Lavender a sidelong glance while she complained, Albert, with practiced ease, helped Van swallow the medicine.

"I learned how to care for the wounded when I served Lady Esta on battlefields."

"Thank you."

Van's shoulders trembled when he met Albert's gaze. Albert smiled at that.

"You feel bad about what you did, don't you?"

"...Do you hate me?"

"Not at all."

Albert's expression stayed tranquil.

"But didn't it hurt?"

"Of course. Enough so that I was sure I'd die." Albert chuckled ruefully.

He stood and made to leave through the door, but stopped and turned around.

"But I won."

Albert stared at the stunned Van for a moment, then lowered his head and exited.

"What's his problem?!" Lavender erupted.

Van thought for a moment.

"Albert was right to act as he did. If he hadn't stopped me, I would have surely ceased to be the Hero. And yet…" Van paused, trying to find the words for his feelings. "Frustration? I feel frustrated at having lost?"

"Van…"

There was concern in Lavender's voice when she saw him looking troubled in a new sort of way.

✳   ✳   ✳

"Behaving yourself, I see. Good, good."

"What is this binding?! I can't break it even with all my strength! What's going on?!"

Lavender wasted no time raising a fuss when she saw me.

"It's a material made ages ago by a wood elf mage to tie a monster whale. It won't break easily."

"Binding me with something like that isn't fair!"

Lavender had been fearsome when fighting Rit and the others, but now she maintained her fairy appearance and personality.

It's because she knows Van isn't in any danger here. I guess that means we'll be all right.

"Lavender, I need to have a chat with Van, so could you wait in another room?"

"What?!"

"We need to talk, just the two of us, in order to clear up Van's confusion."

"Ugh..."

Lavender glanced at Van. After seeing him nod, she sighed.

"Fine... But you better not hurt Van."

"We've fought enough already."

Lavender hopped down from the bed, glared at me for a moment, and then strolled out of the room like she owned the place, despite being tied up.

"You wouldn't know she was bound at all."

I was impressed by how grandly she exited before I closed the door.

"Now then." I set a chair next to Van's bed and sat down. "How are you feeling?"

"...Not great."

There was a sharpness to his tone, and emotion.

That's a good sign.

"I can imagine. Losing to someone you wanted to beat is never fun."

"Says the guy who won."

I laughed out loud at that, and Van smiled a little bit, too.

"That was dirty, Gideon."

"I wanted to win no matter what."

"...I want to fight again."

"We both managed to survive this time, but there are no rematches when it comes to battle."

"…You're only saying that to get out of a rematch."

"I'm glad you understand."

Van laughed with me this time.

"I've never felt this sort of frustration before… Am I a failure as the Hero?"

"How are your impulses?"

"…They returned when I woke up. I won't try to destroy this village again."

Most likely, his rage had blocked his blessing's urges. Typically, that sort of thing was impossible, but I knew of a similar occurrence with Ruti.

"Then I think you have your answer. So long as you possess the Divine Blessing of the Hero, the role God gave you will remain. That's what the church teaches."

Van looked like he couldn't accept that. He'd always followed the church's doctrine, but now he felt unworthy of his blessing. However, that was what it really meant to be the Hero.

"Van, the Hero isn't something to just be. The true Hero is one who strives to live up to the ideal."

"The ideal?"

Shisandan had mentioned something similar once. I didn't like borrowing an enemy's words, but the original Hero had been an Asura demon. As a fellow Asura demon, Shisandan knew the true Hero.

"You aren't a hero because you have the Hero blessing. You become a hero by thinking for yourself about what it means to be one, by occasionally listening to the advice of others, and even by doubting yourself many times. You do it all while pushing forward to reach that ideal."

"Then what should I…?"

"I know what you lack."

"Huh?"

"A mentor."

Van was stunned. I bet he hadn't expected that answer.

"Your whole life has been focused on faith. You don't have enough worldly knowledge or experience."

"Experience…"

"Superior swordsmanship is guided by a philosophy of one kind or another, yet your blade lacks that. It's something that is nurtured through interactions with others, through trying things and considering different ideas."

"A philosophy?"

"Your world is too small, and although your sword is sharp, it's shallow, too… That's why you lost to me."

"…Shallow…"

"You only have one pattern—push through with brute force. A blade like that is easy to disrupt with a counterattack."

"Mrgh?"

Van's boyish face grimaced with his obvious annoyance.

It was a hard expression, quite unlike his former constant air of detachment.

Losing his pure manifestation of the Hero blessing would weaken him for a time. But as he gained more life experience, he'd grow stronger than ever.

In time, he'd probably become the strongest Hero, one in a similar vein to Ruti.

"In the future, you should listen more to what Esta tells you. Not just when it comes to being the Hero, either. You should talk to her about all sorts of things. She has traveled to many countries and seen things that no one else has. There are differences between spears and swords, but it will at least be a point of reference."

"Esta… Is she still willing to travel with me?"

"If you strive to be a hero, then I'm sure she will accompany you. Because she is the hero's guide."

"She's the hero's guide?"

"Not because of her blessing, but because that's what she wants to do. If not, she would've abandoned such a troublesome hero long ago."

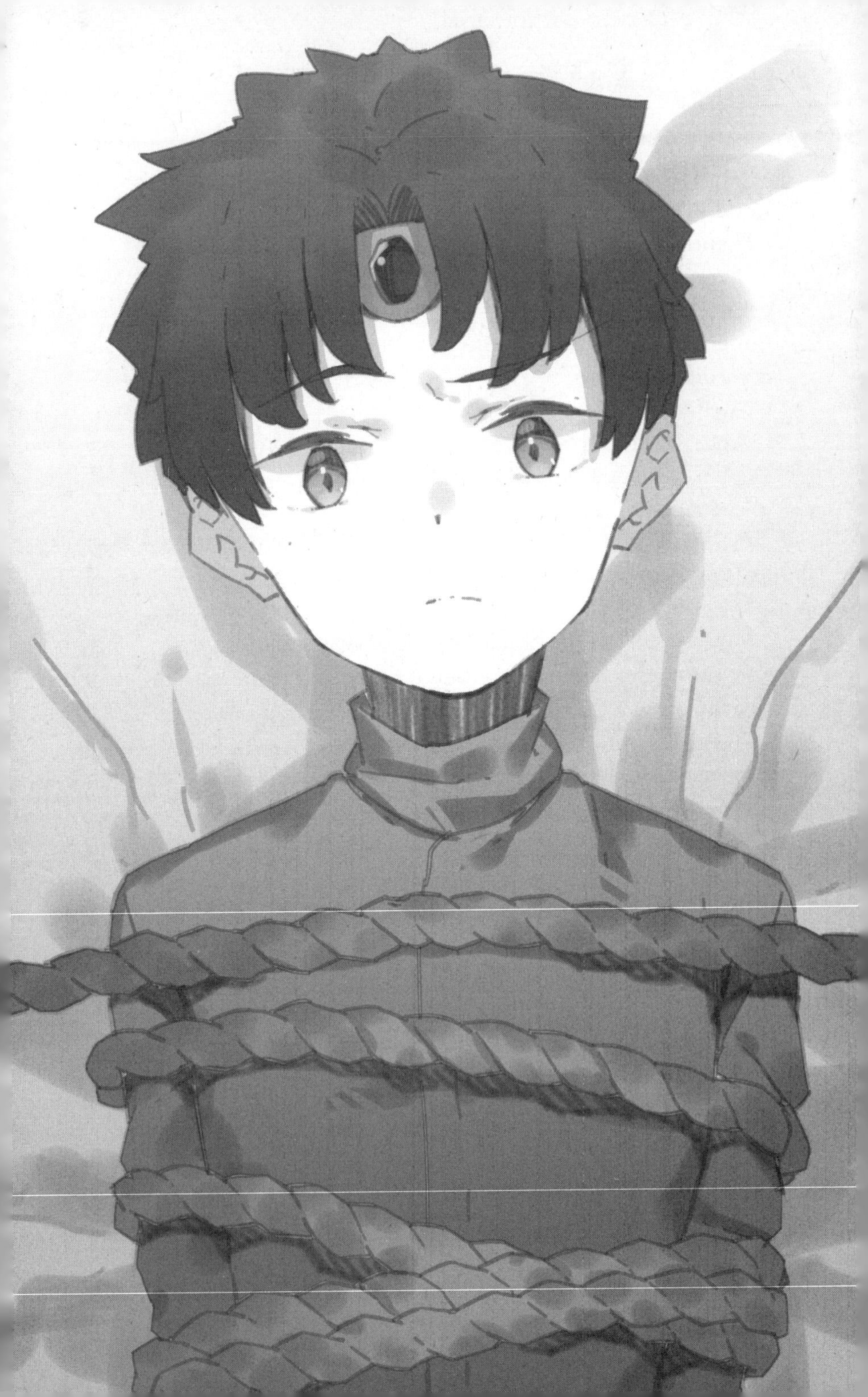

"...That's harsh. But you're probably right." Van went silent for a moment to consider something. "Gideon...would you be willing to come with me?"

"I was Ruti's guide. I don't want to travel with another hero."

"I guess that figures." Van shook his head in disappointment.

A hero, huh...?

I wasn't sure whether to say what I had in mind. There was nothing left to do if I only wanted Van to leave Zoltan. If he was willing to listen to Esta, then she could guide him to become a proper hero.

But...I couldn't help feeling that remaining silent would be wrong, since he would fight as a hero from now on.

"Van, I can't leave Zoltan, but...what do you say to a short adventure with me here?"

"An adventure?"

"Searching some ancient elf ruins."

"Wasn't the ancient elf stuff just made up to hide Ruti?"

"Always stick as close to the truth as possible to make a convincing lie. The bit about an ancient elf creation guarding Zoltan was false, but there are ruins."

"What will we find?"

"I don't know."

"Huh?"

Van was dumbstruck. All of his previous undertakings had been thoroughly investigated beforehand. His adventuring life had been about fighting powerful enemies to raise his level or searching for magic items known to be in certain unexplored regions.

"We'll be investigating in an area where we don't know what we'll encounter."

"Um..."

"It might be worthwhile for you. Those ancient elf ruins are linked to the Hero in some way."

"Really?"

"You never got the proof of the Hero, right?"

"Oh, that treasure said to be sealed in the ancient elf structure near the capital of Avalonia? I thought Ruti already took it."

"Yeah, she did...and I saw how the machine that supposedly sealed the proof of the Hero presented that amulet to her."

"How do you mean?"

"It created the proof of the Hero. The item isn't the same treasure a previous Hero carried, or the amulet written of in ancient legends. The device in the ruins generated an entirely new one for Ruti."

"That's..."

Van was shocked. The proof of the Hero was a fabled treasure, an item that supposedly strengthened the Divine Blessing of the Hero. Hearing that it was some mass-produced object would've struck anyone speechless.

"Basically, the ancient elves had a deep connection with the Hero."

"...And you think there's something to be found in the ruins by Zoltan, too?"

"There is a section in the ruins called the Hero Administration Bureau."

"Hero Administration Bureau?" Van was understandably confused. "What in the world is that?"

"That's what we'd be investigating. I think we might be able to uncover the link between the ancient elves and the Hero—what Divine Blessings are."

"The link..."

After this, Van was going to risk his life fighting the demon lord's army for the sake of the world. I wouldn't join him on that journey, but I still wanted him to set out with no regrets about his decision.

That's why I continued.

"Van...you weren't born with the Hero blessing, were you?"

"?!"

He looked completely taken aback. There was a trace of fear in his eyes that the Hero should have suppressed.

"How did you...?"

"I realized it by observing your ideals."

Van was pure. He had grown up in a monastery, and that was all he knew. Where had that intense purity come from? The obvious answer was that he'd been a deeply pious martyr type to begin with. However, his understanding of the Hero was still too naive.

"If you were always so true to your blessing, then why didn't you leave the monastery the moment the demon lord's army arrived? No, the instant you connected with your blessing? There are always troubled people in the world, after all."

"That's..."

"You didn't act, even as the demon lord's army destroyed your homeland. Why?"

Van looked down. I did my best to maintain a gentle tone as I went on.

"When I considered that, I realized why Ljubo believed you were the Hero."

As self-interested as Cardinal Ljubo had been, why would he risk his reputation by trusting some nameless boy who showed up claiming to be the Hero?

"Ljubo knew you long before that, didn't he? Because your original blessing was Cardinal."

"You're amazing..."

That was why a prince of Flamberge had been sent to the monastery in Avalonia.

"I connected with my blessing at the age of four."

"That's early. And I'm sure you had a high affinity with it, too."

Only people with the Cardinal blessing were allowed to become cardinals of the holy church. So King Flamberge sent Van to the monastery in Avalonia, which was closer to the Last Wall fortress.

"Cardinal Ljubo initially knew you as a future cardinal candidate, a potential recruit for his faction."

"Mhm. I met Cardinal Ljubo twice before I became the Hero. I think that's why he believed me."

"The Cardinal and the Hero are very different blessings. So when he saw you using skills that Cardinal doesn't have access to, he knew you were special even though he couldn't use Appraisal."

A change in blessing. That miracle was why Ljubo had believed that Van was the Hero.

"You lived as a priest, then suddenly had to change your worldview. That's why you became a Hero who blindly followed your faith and your blessing's impulses."

Van's piety surely meant he'd felt great joy at God's miracle yet also been terribly bewildered. Once cut off from the life he had spent living according to his Cardinal blessing, he'd had to begin anew with a completely different blessing.

"I don't know what's waiting in the ancient elf ruins. But I do know that it's somehow connected to the Hero."

"The Hero is a blessing created by God. That's all there is to it..."

"But the first Hero was an Asura demon."

"That can't be true! Asura demons don't have blessings!" Van shook his head.

"But it is."

"I don't know... God exists. God can't possibly be mistaken."

Van looked deeply troubled.

"I won't force you. I only told you because I thought it would be unfair to keep this information from you, knowing that it might have an answer to what the Hero is."

My heart ached a little when I saw Van bite his lip with unease.

Can I really saddle him with the fate of the world?

Unlike Ruti, Van had chosen this fight for himself. It would be wrong to deny his decision. If he intended to be a hero, then I'd support him. That was all there was to it.

"...I want to know what the Hero is, too, and if there's some special meaning to the miracle that occurred."

"I see. Then that settles it."

I undid the ropes tying Van down. He put his right hand to his chest and used Healing Hands.

"Whatever we find in there, try not to take it too seriously," I said.

"That's not really possible after you built it up so much."

"You are you. That won't change whether your blessing is the

Cardinal or the Hero. As long as you don't forget that, I'm sure you'll be fine. Oh, and while we're camping, I want to teach you some basic swordsmanship."

"Swordsmanship… That sounds nice."

The purity in Van's eyes that had caused so many people so much trouble was gone.

The menace of Van the Hero had passed, and with that, our goal had been achieved.

I hoped he'd become a person who strove to be a hero and that his life would be one without regret. And that was why I'd decided to stick around in Van the Hero's story for a little longer.

Our next target was the Hero Administration Bureau.

Afterword

Thank you, everyone who picked up this book! I'm the author, Zappon.

This series has made it to nine volumes. It's on the verge of double digits! Seeing the whole series on the shelf at bookstores is a proud moment. It has a really powerful presence lined up like that.

Also! The anime will begin airing in October 2021!

Remotely, from Kyushu, I took part in the screenplay meetings, sketch work, post-sync, dubbing, and all the stages of the anime production.

The screenplays were taken from the original light novels and Ikeno's manga. They were then worked into storyboards, and the animation created from those was voiced by all the actors, and then the music and sound effects were added. I was able to participate in every stage of the anime's creation.

The images weren't complete at the time, but when I saw my story become a walking, talking anime at the dubbing stage, I forgot that I was working as a member of the production staff and felt utterly stunned by what our work had become.

Apparently, it's rare for an original author to be so deeply involved, but I wanted to participate in the anime's creation as a production staff member rather than as a director. All the staff members got along well and shared opinions openly, maybe because we all wanted to make an interesting anime.

I greatly respect Director Hoshino and the rest of the production team.

When the decision was made to turn *Banished from the Hero's Party* into an anime, my editor warned me that an anime was a happy thing, but also a ton of work. Still, I wound up a very happy author.

The other media adaptations are proceeding smoothly as well!

Volume 7 of the manga is on sale now! It depicts the climax from the second volume of the light novel series!

And the PC game's development is moving along, too. I can't wait to see how it turns out!

Your support is the reason I've become such a happy author. Thank you all so much.

There's no greater joy than knowing all of you who support this series enjoyed this book.

Let's meet again in Volume 10!

Zappon
While listening to the anime's theme song, 2021

This is Yasumo, the illustrator. Thanks for all of your support!

HAVE YOU BEEN TURNED ON TO LIGHT NOVELS YET?

86—EIGHTY-SIX, VOL. 1–11

In truth, there is no such thing as a bloodless war. Beyond the fortified walls protecting the eighty-five Republic Sectors lies the "nonexistent" Eighty-Sixth Sector. The young men and women of this forsaken land are branded the Eighty-Six and, stripped of their humanity, pilot "unmanned" weapons into battle...

Manga adaptation available now!

WOLF & PARCHMENT, VOL. 1–6

The young man Col dreams of one day joining the holy clergy and departs on a journey from the bathhouse, Spice and Wolf. Winfiel Kingdom's prince has invited him to help correct the sins of the Church. But as his travels begin, Col discovers in his luggage a young girl with a wolf's ears and tail named Myuri, who stowed away for the ride!

Manga adaptation available now!

SOLO LEVELING, VOL. 1–8

E-rank hunter Jinwoo Sung has no money, no talent, and no prospects to speak of—and apparently, no luck, either! When he enters a hidden double dungeon one fateful day, he's abandoned by his party and left to die at the hands of some of the most horrific monsters he's ever encountered.

Comic adaptation available now!

THE SAGA OF TANYA THE EVIL, VOL. 1-11

Reborn as a destitute orphaned girl with nothing to her name but memories of a previous life, Tanya will do whatever it takes to survive, even if it means living life behind the barrel of a gun!

Manga adaptation available now!

SO I'M A SPIDER, SO WHAT?, VOL. 1-16

I used to be a normal high school girl, but in the blink of an eye, I woke up in a place I've never seen before and—and I was reborn as a spider?!

Manga adaptation available now!

OVERLORD, VOL. 1-16

When Momonga logs in one last time just to be there when the servers go dark, something happens—and suddenly, fantasy is reality. A rogues' gallery of fanatically devoted NPCs is ready to obey his every order, but the world Momonga now inhabits is not the one he remembers.

Manga adaptation available now!

VISIT YENPRESS.COM TO CHECK OUT ALL OUR TITLES AND...

GET YOUR YEN ON!

Yen ON • Yen Press